Scarred

Confessions of a Single Mum

Jessica Jones

Instagram: **confessionsofasinglemumxx**

Disclaimer:

This book is a work of fiction that's based upon actual facts. In certain cases, incidents, characters and timelines have been changed for dramatic purposes. Certain characters may be composites or entirely fictitious.

ISBN: 978-1-5272-9596-4

Prologue

Nobody is perfect. We all have demons; it is just whether we choose to feed them or not. Here are my demons poured out in the rawest, most honest form. Be gentle with my heart and mind as you read these pages. Be kind with my bravery as I give you uncomfortable truths. There is so much courage in being vulnerable; in showing your soft, sensitive side. Bear that in mind as I hand mine over to you. This is the real me. This is the imperfect, flawed, lost soul I was after becoming single.

Learn me slowly. Please be patient with my pages.

~Pavana Reddy

Contents

My whole life, I have looked to quotes to help me understand my thoughts and feelings. The way I see it, if there is a quote out there that explains exactly how I am feeling, then that must mean I am not alone. I am not the only person who feels this way. I have spent many years searching for understandings and meanings. So, I will continue to show you parts of me through my favourite quotes.

You never know what someone is going through. Be kind always.

~Unknown

You don't have to be in love with someone for your heart to hurt.

Chapter One
The Mountain

You're always one decision away from a totally different life.

~Mark Batterson

My name is Elle Rose Hobson, and at the age of twenty-eight I thought life was perfect. Noah, my son, was two-and-a-half, happy and healthy, my hair salon was expanding rapidly, and I had booked my dream wedding to marry my childhood sweetheart, Chris, in a year. Everything was falling into place.

I was also about to embark on the adventure of a lifetime. I was climbing the world's tallest freestanding mountain, Kilimanjaro, with my best friend, Amy. While raising money for charity, I was ultimately doing this adventure for myself. I wanted to see the world in a different light; from a different view. I couldn't wait to embark on a trip that I knew would change my outlook forever. I just didn't realise how much it would change.

The guy I met on this trip means so much to me. I shared an experience with him that I will remember forever. I will be eternally grateful that we crossed paths at that exact time. I'm a massive believer in fate, that everything happens for a reason; that we meet every single person, whether good or bad, to bring us to exactly where we need to be. This event also brought about the realisation that my life wasn't as perfect as I thought.

Climb mountains not so the world can see you, but so you can see the world.

~David McCullough Jr

After months of preparation, the day came to leave our lives behind for just over two weeks and face this mammoth expedition. As my seemingly lousy luck goes, we had to turn the car around on the way to the airport because I forgot my passport. Then, true to form, we got held up at border control because apparently, my passport wasn't in good enough condition to fly. *Great, all that training for nothing!* Thankfully the heavens were on my side that day, and we got the all-clear just one minute before the check-in closed. Stressed, sweaty and with eyes full of tears of joy, we raced through security to the departure lounge.

Since booking our trip, Amy and I had been part of a WhatsApp group with four other people who'd also be doing the climb with us. We chatted about training, medication and what to pack. Knowing what they looked like from their profile pictures, we were like two meerkats, trying to find them through the crowds at Heathrow. Then, there they were: Jack and Reece, seeming to part the crowds as they came to say hello. You couldn't really miss Jack, towering over the other people with a walk that said he didn't have a care in the world. He was a perfectly put-together Scouser. That summed them up; two of the most laidback guys I had ever met – quite the contrast to Amy and me, two blonde bimbos running around like headless chickens thinking we were about to miss our flight. We had no idea that these men were about to change our lives beyond belief.

We meet no ordinary people in our lives.

~C.S. Lewis

Three airports, two flights and a long Jeep ride later, we were like two giggling schoolgirls by the time we got to our hotel. Instantly there was a bond between the four of us, and I quickly felt at ease that we had these two men to lean on if we were struggling or needed cheering up when we were missing home. We had two days of getting to know them before we set off on the ascent and were stripped of the outside world, as our phones didn't work outside the hotel. Since I was thirteen years old, I don't think I've ever been without my phone for more than a day or two, so I knew it was going to be hard – never mind the mountain we were going to climb. We said our goodbyes to our friends and family and set off in another Jeep to take us to the bottom of the mountain. From the get-go, everyday life became a distant memory as I was so anxious and scared about what the next eight days would bring. I couldn't think of anything else.

The first day and night were pretty easy compared to what lay ahead. It was only three hours of walking and not that high, so we acclimatised nicely to the altitude. After our first dinner in camp, the other two people in our group got themselves an early night, and the four of us were left in the dinner tent. We stayed up for hours (I know, not what you're supposed to do when you're climbing Kilimanjaro), but it was as if we were on a school trip – non-stop laughter, playing games, telling stories and getting to know each other. We probably didn't take it as seriously as we should have, which was all the more apparent the following morning when we were awoken at six o'clock with a bowl of water for us to shower.

The following day, Jack and I naturally started to walk with each other as our pace was faster than the others. I was fascinated by him. I quickly came to realise that we were worlds apart, from entirely opposite upbringings and lives, but it didn't stop us from talking about everything and anything. I started to understand how people on reality shows feel so deeply for their co-stars within days of knowing each other because they're isolated from the world and can only see what is in front of them. Many a time, I've been sat at home thinking *OMG, these people are crazy. How can they form relationships and friendships like that after such a short time?!* But you really are in a bubble, and it's so rare to be in such situations that when you are, you see people in such a different light and what you see is what you get. You aren't distracted by mobile phones, by social media, by work. You are quite literally living in the moment and getting to know someone for their true self.

Sometimes the greatest adventure is simply a conversation.

~Amadeus Wolfe

Day three hit us real hard – eight hours of slugging through a blistering snowstorm, walking through waterfalls that had sprung to life in the heavy downpours.

Amy broke first and slumped on a rock, crying that she couldn't go any further. I wiped away her tears and fed her energy gels. We had two hours to go until our next camp, and the weather was worse than ever. We were completely soaked from head to toe, couldn't feel our fingers or toes, and our heads were pounding from the altitude. We were both probably minutes away from giving up, and then Jack and Reece came to our rescue, offering to carry our bags to relieve at least some of the weight. Jack not only supported me physically, but mentally too. Time seemed to be slowing down as the weather was appalling, and I felt like I didn't have an ounce of energy to even string a sentence together. When you start to feel down on that mountain, it is treacherous. But Jack would stand over me, wipe away my tears, kiss my forehead, grab my face and tell me everything would be OK and that we were all going to get up this mountain, no matter what.

As the long, exhausting days went on, Jack quickly became someone I looked up to and looked forward to seeing – even when we'd only said goodnight to each other hours before. He became my rock. Jack made sure I was eating the right amount of food and the right types to avoid aggravating my allergies whilst not seeming to give himself a second thought. Well, maybe that's not entirely true, because he made sure everyone knew if he didn't like the food. But Jack thought about me first, and if it wasn't good enough he would make sure it was. He seemed to care so much about me and my needs. I couldn't believe how close I had gotten to this person who'd been a stranger just a week ago. He is also, without a doubt, one of the funniest people I've ever met. He had us in stitches, all day and all night. He would sing to cheer us up, he would sing to wake us up, and he would sing to annoy the hell out of us. I have never met anyone like him in my life. He was like a firefly, lighting up the room (or the fresh outdoors, I should say).

On day five, we walked past a gigantic signal tower. I tried my luck and called Noah but I didn't know where or who he was with. It took four phone calls to finally hear that little voice I was so desperate to hear. He could barely string a sentence together at the time but managed to say "miss you", and that was enough. Jack and I were walking together the second we got a signal. He walked off to give me space to make the phone call, and then he was right there when I needed him afterwards to pick up the pieces. He just held me tightly, not saying a word as a mix of happy and sad tears streamed down my face.

The following evening we would reach base camp but that night and the one after were two of the worst nights of my life. We went to bed around six o'clock in the evening and were woken five hours later to have "breakfast" before setting off at midnight. Amy and I struggled to get out of our sleeping bags, saying we didn't know whether we could do this. The nerves started kicking in, and I couldn't eat a single thing. The altitude sickness had begun to get to me the last couple of days, and I was losing my appetite more and more. But Jack was telling me

I needed to eat something and practically forced eggs and energy bars down me before we took off.

The four of us stuck together for the majority of the summit. There was Jack who nearly shit himself, Liam who barely spoke two words the entire time, Amy who had to sit on a rock every ten minutes because she thought her brain was swelling, and me, projectile vomiting along the pathway. It was horrific.

After six hours of walking the sun began to rise, which meant we were only a few hours from the summit. We all had a little rest when this happened. We shared a group hug, took some photos and really made the most of the unbelievable view that we would probably never see again. It was all so surreal; not many words were exchanged as we all started to get really short of breath, but you could see in everyone's eyes how magical that moment was.

Travel opens your heart, broadens your mind and fills your mind with stories to tell.

~Paula Bendfeldt

I can't explain the emotions when you make it to the top of that mountain. The last hour we all started to stagger; Amy's heart rate was well above normal and to make matters worse, twenty minutes from the top we walked past a dead body. The walkway was so narrow that our feet practically brushed the foil blanket that the poor man lay underneath. My anxiety was at an all-time high, tears started rolling down my face, and I remember telling myself I would never make it. You are so close but still feel so far away – every step gets more demanding than the last.

After what felt like a lifetime, I finally made it to the top. I made it first because I was so close to my guide's feet. It's all I could concentrate on without thinking I was going to have a heart attack. After about five minutes at the top on my own, I hurled over the wooden sign, not sure if I was going to be sick or faint, and I saw Jack coming up towards me. We grabbed hold of each other and burst into tears. "We made it, " we mumbled to each other. Amy and Reece were just five minutes behind, and the second we saw one another, it was as if it was a reunion of not seeing each other for ten years. We wailed in each other's arms, screaming: "We fucking did it, babe!"

I thought that the worst was over, but it wasn't. We reached the summit at eight o'clock in the morning, the minus-twenty-degree blizzard making it almost impossible to stay at the top for longer than ten minutes.

On the way back down, Amy thought it would be a good idea to ski down on our bums. I mean, it was a great idea in that it took us half the time, however adjusting to the rapid change in altitude wasn't good, and I vomited everywhere – including once over Amy's shoulders.

We eventually got back to base camp at around two o'clock in the afternoon and were reunited with the rest of the group. We were only allowed to sleep for a couple of hours before we were woken up to walk another four hours down to a different camp where we were fed and got more sleep.

Maybe it was the accomplishment of reaching the top, the team effort or the fact I couldn't have done it without him, but the experience drew me closer to Jack. He was like my safety net, and I craved his affection and warmth. If he saw me stop on the way down, he would run back towards me, cuddle me and ask me if I was OK, readjusting my bag straps and making sure I was drinking lots of water.

There's something to be said for people who genuinely make you feel safer. Even if they're far away from you, their existence is so calming and beautiful, that it makes everything seem better somehow.

~Unknown

That evening we ate like kings and queens, reminiscing on the entire climb that now felt so long ago. Later on, tucked up in our sleeping bags, Amy and I spoke for hours. I don't know how the hell we had the energy, we were so drained and emotional, but the conversation got very deep.

"Why the hell am I not missing my fiancé?" I asked Amy, as if she would know the answer. "Why do I not want to go home?" I was almost begging for an answer. I was starting to wonder, *do I have romantic feelings towards Jack?* But I knew deep down that I saw him as a big brother; more like a guardian angel, actually. I didn't have the urge to kiss him or anything, so why did I doubt my relationship back home if it wasn't because of someone else? Perhaps blaming it on someone else made it easier, but that wasn't it.

The following morning, I woke up to the astounding screech of Amy shouting, "Fuck, Elle, you need to go to the hospital, babe, your face has blown up!"

To my horror, I had reacted to the altitude and my face, from eyelids to lips, had swelled up. Later, when my lips and nose started to blister, I found out I also had severe frostbite. *Brilliant.* If I hadn't already been insecure about my looks, I sure was then. I went to breakfast with my entire face covered, hiding the tears that wouldn't stop coming, but it was Jack that somehow still made me feel beautiful.

It was the last stint of the walk down, which on average takes six hours, but the four of us did it in just over three. We were so ready to be off that godforsaken mountain and get a shower and a beer. Plus, there was the fact I needed medical help pretty urgently with my lips full of pus and blood.

For the rest of that last walk, Jack regularly checked on me: pulling down the balaclava that was sheltering my blistered lips from the sun, telling me that everything was going to be OK and kissing me on the forehead. He said we would get help and go to the doctor as soon as we were back. I don't tend to listen to people and I usually only think about what I want to believe, but Jack's reassurance felt authentic. I felt safe with him and I believed that everything was going to be OK. If it had just been Amy and me, I would have been crying the entire way down telling her my face was going to drop off, and no doubt she would have laughed and agreed.

Jack's long legs got him down to the finish line first, and I came tumbling down around twenty minutes later. He had a beer and a Diet Coke waiting for me. He picked me up, swung me around and told me how proud he was that we had finally completed it. I burst into tears at the thought of someone being so proud of me. I can honestly say, hand on my heart, that I wouldn't have been able to make it up that mountain without Jack. Of course, I wouldn't have been able to make it up there without Amy either. She was like my soul sister, my blood brother, my twin up there, and Reece too, but with Jack, it was different, and I don't think I would have made it past day three without him.

We headed back to the hotel after a short stop at the hospital, where I was given antibiotics. I was in agony and could barely speak, let alone eat or drink. The pus was worsening by the second as I prayed for the medication to kick in. It felt so good to dive into a long-awaited and much-needed shower before making our way to the celebration party with our guides. Then our group went out for a meal – it was as if we were trying to consume all the calories we burned off in the last eight days in one sitting! I sat there, drinking through a straw and managing to just eat enough to keep me going.

At the end of the evening, we made our way back to our hotel and the four of us stayed up until two in the morning. I had never felt so exhausted in my entire life, but I could have stayed up all night long. Jack and Reece were leaving for the

UK the next day and the thought of them going was heartbreaking. I didn't want them to leave because it meant this adventure was coming to an end and that I was a step closer back to normality and real life; something that was starting to terrify me.

Travel isn't always pretty. It isn't always comfortable. Sometimes it hurts, it even breaks your heart. But that's okay. The journey changes you– it should change you.

~Anthony Bourdain

The next morning, we ran into the men's room and jumped on their beds, cuddling them and telling them how much we didn't want them to go, to not get their flights and to stay and do the volunteer work with us. But of course, they had to go.

When they'd gone, it was like a part of us had left too. Amy and I were miserable. We were feeling all of our emotions at once, so we decided to laze around the swimming pool and get drunk on cheap beer. It really was like we were heartbroken, and that's when I understood that you don't have to be in love with someone for your heart to hurt.

It was the fear of maybe never seeing these incredible men again. The pain that this unbelievable experience was coming to an end. Of course, this was no love story. Going through something that is so physically and mentally challenging changes you regardless. It makes you see things you never thought you would see and learn things about yourself you never knew. I had all these sudden doubts and worries spiralling around my head about my relationship at home, but it wasn't until I was back on British soil that everything became clear.

Maybe we were the right people at the wrong time. Maybe we just met each other too young. Maybe…

Chapter Two
The Ending and the Beginning

Don't forget: somewhere between hello and goodbye, there was love, so much love.

~Faraway

After three airports and a sixteen-hour flight, it felt like it took days to get home. I couldn't believe I still had tears left to cry. But I did – and a lot. My lips were still in agony, and every salty tear that fell made them sting that little bit more. We finally landed at Gatwick at eight-thirty in the morning, and I thought: *This is it – the moment of truth.* Then my phone rang. It was my dad.

"Hi poppet, I've just parked. I'll see you in five minutes."

"I've texted and rung Chris, but I've had no reply. He's with you, isn't he?" I asked my dad.

"No, he's not."

"You're joking, aren't you? Surely he's with you?" I said as my heart started to race.

"Erm… long story, sweetheart, I'll see you in five minutes, OK?"

OMG, he's going to pretend he hasn't come and he's going to surprise me with something. The man I knew and loved. A banner, balloons, to run in with Noah, anything!

The excitement started to rush through my body as we collected our bags and rushed to arrivals. But there was my dad, standing alone. I dropped my bags and ran, throwing my arms around him and squeezing him as if we hadn't seen each other in years, tears rushing down my face.

"I'm so, so proud of you, Elle. You made it, my girl."

But I couldn't concentrate. My eyes were scanning the terminal for any sign of Chris.

"Where's Chris?" I said.

"He's still in bed asleep. He didn't want to get up. I'm so sorry, " he said nervously.

For a second, I think my heart stopped. It felt like someone had ripped it out of my chest and stood on it. Again and again and again.

"What do you mean he didn't want to get up?"

"His alarm went off three or four times, and we knocked on the door numerous times, but he told me to come without him."

I had no words, staring at my dad, eyes glazed, thinking, *this can't be happening.*

"Let's just get in the car, hey? Amy's got another flight to catch, " my dad said calmly.

We dropped Amy off at Terminal 5 to get her connecting flight. Our goodbye was like no goodbye I have ever had before. Anyone in that airport who saw us must have thought we were never going to see each other again, as we hugged and kissed each other goodbye after an experience of a lifetime.

Within two minutes of getting back into my dad's car, I burst into tears, blubbing: "I don't want to marry him, Dad."

It might seem strange to start a story with an ending, but all endings are also beginnings. We just don't know it at the time.

~Mitch Alborn

Chris was the love of my life. My childhood sweetheart, the man I dreamt of settling down with, marrying and being with forever. The man whose heart I broke but who also broke mine in so many ways. The man that still means more to me than all these men in this book. This is a chapter about a relationship breaking down. Two kids who fell in love but slowly grew into two different people and wanted different things out of life. There is love there, so much love, but it's love lost.

I first set eyes on Chris when I was sixteen. He was the most beautiful man I'd ever seen. He was tall, dark, and had the world's most perfect lips and dazzling green eyes. We went to the same secondary school, but he had a long-term girlfriend when we first met. A couple of years later, it just so happened that we both enrolled at the same college to do the same course… and that's where it all started.

Within weeks we were drawn to each other. We got on brilliantly, and soon enough, Chris left his girlfriend. What made it all the more exciting was that he didn't want to be seen to be moving on that quickly, so we had to keep things under wraps at first. But he couldn't deny his feelings towards me. We would secretly hold hands in the back of the car, and he would wink at me across the table while playing footsie during lunch breaks.

I fell in love with Chris like lightning; fast and all of a sudden. I know I was only sixteen, but I'd already had my fair share of boyfriends and nothing compared. I had absolutely no filter when I was around him. I never got embarrassed, I was never anyone else, I was always myself. He was the funniest person I had ever met. He was the type of person who told little white lies when telling a story to make it sound that extra bit interesting but killed himself laughing when someone pulled him up on it, and he had the most infectious laugh. He quickly became my best friend, someone I told everything to, and even faster became someone I didn't want to live without.

From the first moment that we touched, your arms felt like home.

~John Mark Green

***

As the years went on, there were a lot of things we didn't do because we were together. He got offered a football scholarship in the US but turned it down because he didn't want to leave me. I yearned to go travelling, but Chris wasn't keen so I never went. I almost didn't go to university because I didn't want to be away from him, but we both knew it was what I needed to do. Even so, I chose the one closest to home.

In my second year at university, things started to change. I had never given Chris a reason not to trust me, ever. I came home every weekend, and sometimes during the week, he would travel forty miles to see me. But this is where our lives started to differ. I was growing more independent, meeting new people, going on netball tours, and he was living his same life with the same friends back home.

Like most people, I got a taste for alcohol at university, and Chris didn't drink. Not a sip, nothing. He had grown up around heavy drinkers, and, quite frankly, he never liked the taste. Whenever I had a drink, even if I was just a little tipsy, he would jump to conclusions and accuse me of being wasted, which was frustrating. It was probably the first thing that we really butted heads on because we looked at it from different viewpoints.

To make matters worse, I took up smoking – another thing Chris disliked. Half of the people I lived with smoked and, admittedly, I have an addictive personality, so once I tried it, I didn't want to stop. To avoid arguments, I would hide the habit from Chris when I was home with countless packets of chewing gum and cheap perfume.

Before I knew it, we were living two quite different lives. The more I started to go out, the less I texted Chris. I was too busy letting my hair down. Understandably he started texting me more, asking why I wasn't replying, but I found that irritating like he was pestering me. I was too busy downing shots with friends, singing my heart out and dancing up poles in student bars – typical university stuff. He was starting to push me away, and I felt trapped. Everyone around me was single, and I felt like I was missing out. I told him we needed a break.

One night, I got drunk and kissed a guy. It was the first time in four years I had kissed anyone else, but I quickly got an appetite for being single and all the attention that came with it, so I ended my relationship with Chris after a two-week break. I was twenty years old and told myself I wanted the freedom to live my life. But it wasn't really that. I was really into this other guy. It was just something new and exciting. He was a rugby player, two years older than me, oozed confidence and was so goddamn beautiful.

Having graduated from university that year, he moved back to London, and we both found the distance too hard, so it was over before it began. After just eight weeks of being separated from Chris, I heard that he was seeing someone. I couldn't believe it. He was so heartbroken when I ended it. I thought he would never move on. I had this ache in my heart – even though I didn't want him, I didn't want anyone else to have him. I couldn't help myself, so I reached out, begged him to see me. Within a day of our meeting, he called it off with the other girl. And just like that, we were back on.

Souls tend to go back to who feels like home.

~N.R. Hart

It was just like when we first met. Sneaking around, going on dates, it was all so exciting. But as the weeks went on, I started to hear rumours that Chris had slept with lots of different women when we weren't together. I thought, *this can't be true, not my Chris? I was only the second person he had slept with. He isn't like that?* With my heart racing, I asked him to tell me everything. He told me there had been five girls. It was like taking a bullet. I cried and cried and cried. I could NOT get the images of him fucking other women out of my head. I didn't want to end things, but I couldn't stand the thought of him touching me or going near me for a long time.

One night I got talking to his brother's girlfriend and confessed that I knew about the women and how awful it made me feel. "I couldn't believe the girls he brought home, Elle. When Holly Brown walked through the door, we were all shocked."

What?! Who the fuck is Holly Brown? She wasn't on the list of girls he told me about!

I called him out on it the second he walked through the door and he confessed that there had been another three. *Three*! So that meant *eight* women in eight weeks. He told me he didn't want to tell me there were eight because he knew how much it would hurt me. I kept thinking, how is that even possible? How could he have that in him? He sobbed and sobbed, telling me that it was the only way he could get over me, to have sex with other women, to try and fill the void that I'd left.

I don't know why I did it to myself, but for months I searched through all eight girls' Instagram profiles, stalking them daily, trying to visualise how he'd had sex with them. I loved him so much, but I hated him more. I couldn't get past it.

I ended up cheating on him on my twenty-first birthday. He never cheated on me, and he never would have. What he did to me was nothing on the scale of what I did to him. He wasn't even with me when he slept with those girls. But here I was, committing the ultimate betrayal while we were together. The following morning, I came home to find his kitchen filled with balloons and a puppy he'd bought me. The guilt was eating away at me and soon became unbearable, so I ended up confessing what I'd done later that night, telling him I regretted every single second of it.

I thought he would split up with me, tell me how much of an evil bitch I was, that he never wanted to see me again, that it was over. But he didn't. With floods of tears, he begged for it not to be over and that he would forgive me, and everything would be fine.

Sometimes good people make bad choices. It doesn't mean they're bad. It simply means they're human.

~Sui Ishida

I had just three months left at university before I graduated, and things were so different. I'd lost my respect for Chris. I had broken our trust and used it against him. He was worse than ever when I was out drinking, messaging me non-stop. He had every right to be the way he was, but again it pushed me away.

During the last week of term, I broke up with Chris again. I knew in the back of my mind that if I cheated on him, there must be a reason behind it, and I was terrified I would do it to him again. He deserved so much better than that. After five years, I decided we just weren't right for each other at that moment in time. We both needed to go off and do our own thing, live our lives differently and apart.

I'll see you when the road decides it's time for our paths to cross again.

~Ben Maxfield

After we broke up, I met Max (more about him later), and Chris met a beautiful girl called Lily. They had been together for just a few months when things went south with Max. I turned up outside Chris's house and told him I wanted to talk. I was sure that if I asked to get back together, he would come in a heartbeat. But I didn't want him. I just didn't want anyone else to have him, *again*. I was being so heartless and not thinking of him at all.

The next day he broke it off with Lily, but I told him I couldn't get back together with him as I had decided to go travelling to the States in less than a month. It was something I needed to do for me.

What happened next shocked me to my core. I had only been in the US for a matter of weeks when I found out Chris was in a relationship with one of my friends, Becky. My *friend*. This was a girl whose house I had slept at two nights before I left. I didn't know who I hated more. Was this the karma that I deserved for doing what I did to him? For completely shattering his heart and not really giving a fuck? I had enough going on at the time with my own heartbreak (*again, I'll get to this later*) that I let it lie. I wanted him to be happy, so I let him be. For a while, anyway.

I spent six months in America, and when I got home, it wasn't long before I bumped into Chris and Becky. My friends suggested Becky and I talk outside to clear the air, so off we went to have a little girly chat. She really was Becky with the good hair.

We both had our backs up, digging at each other from the get-go. Becky said that Chris and I were history, and that I meant nothing to him now. I felt word vomit burning my throat and I needed to spit it out. The only way to defend myself was to shut her down.

"If he felt so much for you, then why was he messaging me in January when you had been together a month, saying how much he missed me, that he couldn't live without me, that he wanted to get a flight out to see me?"

It was pure evil. Why couldn't I just take it like a champ and accept that they had something special? It worked, though. Becky stormed inside and locked herself in the toilets crying, and that was my cue to leave. I didn't see them again for four months, but I heard through the grapevine that Chris and Becky had been on the rocks for a while. The week they split up, I was outside a bar waiting for my friends one night when I spotted Chris walking towards the queue. I was so embarrassed: one, I was on my own and two, I was smoking. I dove for cover and managed to avoid him.

When my friends arrived, I nervously told them Chris was inside. I couldn't avoid him any longer as the second we walked up to the bar, he was stood on the other side. Every time he looked at me, I looked away and vice versa. This went on for much of the night until his friend came over.

"Are you two going to talk then? You know he's never stopped loving you. He only got with Becky to try and get over you. Now you're back, he just can't be with her."

And that was it. Off we went home in a taxi home together, and within weeks we were back together. Again.

You were home, and I don't know how to not go home.

~Leo Christopher

This time it felt different. I thought it would be third time lucky. This had got to be it. It wasn't long before Chris moved in with me at my parents' house. It was all so exciting again. We'd been apart for more than a year, and it was like falling in love all over again with someone new. Except it wasn't someone new, it was my best friend that I'd just lost for a while. It took some time to finally make peace with the past – both mine and his – and when we did, I never gave his exes or past flings a second thought. Finally, after years of torturing myself, I accepted that this man was completely and utterly obsessed with me and wanted just me. I could do anything, and he still would be head over heels for me. He loved me so much he was willing to give me another chance after I broke his heart twice before.

But if you want to get it right this time, it's going to take all of your heart.

~Seeker

That first year back together was even better than when we were at college. Chris had started to drink (I drove him to it after I broke up with him the second time), so we could finally go out for grown-up nights out. We saved and went travelling in Australia, all the way up the east coast. We were so in love. *This is it,* I thought. *This is it for good.* I wanted to settle, and I couldn't and didn't want to see myself with anyone else. Maybe we were the right people at the wrong time. Maybe we just met each other too young. Maybe… But at the time, I really believed it was right.

Life seemed pretty perfect, but then November came and it was one of the most challenging months of my life. One night my parents sat Chris and me down in their living room. I knew something serious was coming because whenever my mum feels awkward in serious situations, her coping mechanism is to laugh – something I have inherited from her. I thought my parents were getting a divorce or that they had won the lottery (here's to hoping!).

Mum told us she had cancer. I felt like someone had ripped my heart out and torn it to shreds right in front of my face. Her mastectomy was booked for the first week of December. We were still living with my parents, and I can only describe that time as dull and ghost-like. I would lie in bed with my mum most nights as she poured her feelings out, telling me, "This is it." This was the second time she had had cancer, and she was scared she wouldn't survive it again.

Chris was incredible and cared for us both. I couldn't bear the thought of losing my mum. It was like a pain I don't even want to think about. I couldn't tell her that though; I kept putting a brave face on and telling her everything would be okay. In reality, I had no idea if things were ever going to be okay again.

At the time, my acne was so bad I wouldn't leave the house without layers and layers of foundation. I would cry in agony when I got home at the pain and soreness of removing inches of makeup and how ugly I felt. It was the stress from mum being ill that made it flare up, but let's face it, what's acne compared to cancer?

Christmas was just two weeks away. It was a week after mum's operation, and Chris told me he had a secret: he'd booked time off work (mine and his), and he was taking me away. He told me to pack my best attire and go and get my nails done. I couldn't help but feel guilty because I didn't want to leave mum. Chris had never taken me away as a surprise. He had never done anything like this before. Mum persuaded me to go and said that she'd be waiting for me when I got back.

Chris took to me to Paris, a place that had been on my bucket list for years. We went to the top of the Eiffel Tower, where he got down on one knee and proposed with the biggest rock I've ever seen. As marriage proposals go, it was pretty perfect in every detail, from the location right down to the bottle of bubbly waiting for us at the hotel and the big white book he presented to me – each page with love-filled messages from our friends and family. He had exceeded every expectation I had, and I really couldn't have loved him anymore if I tried.

When we arrived home, life was pretty hectic. We had a lot planned for my mum's sixtieth birthday a week before Christmas, then had a busy festive period before we went away as a family for New Year's Eve. I never told my mum this, but I remember looking across the table and thinking how pale and ill she looked. We wanted to make everything as perfect as we could for her, make her realise how loved she was and that we were all here for her.

January came around fast as it always does, and mum started radiotherapy. I ended up quitting my job because they wouldn't give me any more time off. I wanted to be there for her every waking second and I was. I won't ever be able to shake the flashbacks of holding back her hair while she was throwing up and cuddling her until she fell asleep some afternoons when she was exhausted. Yet, she still went to work most days and pretended everything was normal. She's the bravest and strongest woman I know.

After nearly two months of radiotherapy, Mum got the all-clear and life seemed to pick up where it left off. Chris and I started to look for our first home and decided to enjoy our engagement rather than rush to get married. Following the all-clear from the doctor, my mum had to go on what she calls her "cancer tablets" – medication which stops your body from producing oestrogen. Experts usually suggest taking these for five years, but for mum, they recommended taking them for ten years as a preventative measure. After a few weeks of taking the tablets we went out for dinner for some mother-daughter time.

"I won't survive it if I get it a third time, Elle."

The more wine we gulped, the deeper the conversation got, and she started to sob because she feared never being a grandmother. That conversation is all it took for me to know that I didn't want my mum to miss out. Chris would have had children in the years before this. He is such a family man and was always absolutely incredible with children. He would have had a child with me at eighteen if I'd agreed; it has always been something that I have adored about him. It was a no brainer for him when I told him I wanted to have a baby.

It took two months to fall pregnant. Mum was overwhelmed at our news and over the moon.

Chris couldn't have been better while I was pregnant. He was so excited, forever wanting to feel the baby kick. However, pregnancy didn't agree with me. I was severely sick the first few months, and then I was in and out of the hospital every other week. When I was thirty-five weeks I had my third water infection, but this time it had spread to my blood, and we had the scare that they might have to get the baby out there and then, five weeks early. After close examination, the baby was absolutely fine and we were allowed to go home. Just ten days later, at thirty-six weeks and five days, I went into labour and, after thirty hours, ended up having an emergency C-section.

When they finally delivered our darling little boy, they had to take him away for a while as he had a lot of mucus on his chest because he was early. Those ten minutes felt like a lifetime, and Chris just sat there with his lips pressed to my forehead, stroking my hair in complete silence. Then they brought our baby boy back and handed him to Chris. I don't think I can begin to describe the feeling I felt at that very moment. It was as if my life was complete. Seeing him hold Noah, at that moment, I couldn't love him anymore.

You have a place in my heart no one else ever could have.

~F. Scott Fitzgerald

We were allowed to take our little prince home three days later, and Chris couldn't have helped me more if I'd wanted him to. He wanted to be involved in every parenting aspect, exceeding my expectations of what a great dad he would be. Three weeks after giving birth my caesarean incision split open, which sent me back to the hospital, leaving Chris to look after Noah and make the transition of boob to bottle alone. I was devastated I couldn't breastfeed any longer, but Noah was healthy and in all honesty, began to sleep like an angel now he wasn't attached to me. We had our first Christmas in our own home with both families and our perfect boy.

I guess you can't stay on cloud nine forever, though, and as the new year came around, I started to see small changes in Chris. He had stopped taking pride in his appearance and made every excuse as to why he couldn't shift the weight he had gained – he didn't like healthy food and said that going to the gym took too much time away from Noah. The weight thing never bothered me. I loved Chris for Chris, whether he was thirteen stone or sixteen stone, but his lack of motivation was starting to get to me.

He also began to despise his job. Now each night he came home, he wanted to put his feet up within seconds of walking into the house, leaving me to carry on doing all the chores. On the occasions he went out with his friends, he became someone I didn't know. He had always been soppy when he got drunk, telling me how much he loved me, telling me how much he missed me and couldn't wait to come home, but these times I wouldn't hear a peep from him. I don't think it was anything more than being with his friends, but things were changing between us, and I didn't like who he was becoming.

Things got rapidly worse, so I decided to write him a letter. I told him that I was thinking of leaving him because I didn't think he was happy in our relationship anymore. I didn't really intend to give him the letter straight away but I was stupid enough to leave it on the shelf where I thought it was hidden. He went berserk; shouting and asking why, after all these years, could I not communicate with him, why was he so easy to just give up on, and how could I walk away so easily?

We spent the rest of that evening screaming at each other and crying to each other in equal doses. It was a real rollercoaster. I told Chris that what hurt me most was that he never kissed me when he walked through the door. Such a little gesture like that would make all the difference. The thing is, I don't care about diamond rings and fancy shit. Money doesn't mean anything to me, and I would rather be swung around the kitchen or carried up the stairs by the man I love than have him walk through the front door with a pair of Louboutin's.

Chris promised me that he would change, that he would be better. He promised to appreciate me more. To respect me more. To make me feel more wanted and loved.

And he did… for a while.

I was torn between holding on to what you promised and accepting the reality of you not being able to deliver.

~R. H. Sin

That summer we went on two beautiful holidays. Chris and I had our ups and downs, but mostly I felt content and secure, so we decided after three years of being engaged to finally book our wedding. I was tied up for months on end after that, organising and planning. He said he would do whatever I wanted, said that whatever made me happy made him happy. What he said and what he did, however, were two different things. It had been less than a year since our heart-to-heart, and just as Noah was turning two, I started to see those little changes creep back in.

I watched Chris play football every week. Every Saturday and most Tuesdays, I would take Noah to watch him play, and I never missed a home game. Even though most weeks I was busy with my work, I would still drive like a crazy lady to catch the last ten minutes of his game. But when it came to my netball games on Sunday mornings, there was always an excuse.

"It's too early."

"There's no one there to talk to."

"It's too far away to drag Noah there."

Not one game that whole season did he come and watch.

Before, he would come along to concerts with me to see my favourite artist, even if he didn't like them that much. Now, if he didn't enjoy it, he wouldn't do it – even if it was something I loved. I wanted to take walks, see new places, go on adventures just the three of us, make memories – little things. Sundays were the only day we had together as a family, but every single week it was the same old thing. We went over to our friends for food, or they came to our house and we sat and watched a film and ate our body weight in snacks and treats. Don't get me wrong, I did love this. We were such social butterflies and had many couples we loved spending time with, but I couldn't imagine my life being this for another ten years. I felt like we were wasting all this precious time we had with Noah while he was young, and the repetitiveness was boring me to death.

Day by day, Chris's negativity towards the world got worse. Every evening I started to feel anxious that he would get home in a bad mood and little disagreements turned into major rows. I felt like I couldn't even make him dinner without him turning his nose up at it or there being a complaint. I tried to make an effort and cuddle him or jump on him at the door just for a kiss, but he always had an excuse – he was tired, or his back hurt, or he was too hot and sweaty to cuddle. We'd always had a great sex life, but I no longer felt loved outside the bedroom, so that also started to fall by the wayside too. There were nights that he didn't even kiss me goodnight. He wouldn't even say goodnight, he'd just turn his back and go to sleep.

You are not a doormat for someone else's negativity.

~Unknown

Before I knew it, it was the week before I was leaving for the climb. I felt anxious about the whole thing and was having regular panic attacks and migraines. Just days before I was due to set off, Chris told me not to go, that it wasn't worth the stress and I should just stay at home with him and Noah. He wasn't excited for me. He didn't think it was an experience of a lifetime. He just didn't get it.

Friday came, the night before I was leaving. We were going out for a family meal with my parents. I thought I ought to make an effort, as I hadn't all week. It was also going to be the last time I wore makeup or got dolled up for a while, so I got dressed up to the nines. I dressed Noah, and Chris kept him entertained downstairs while I finished getting ready. "I'm just brushing my teeth. I'll be ready in two minutes, " I said. Chris got Noah fixed in his car seat and waited by the door to lock up behind me. I walked down the stairs slowly in my five-inch heels and stared at Chris, but he didn't glance up, not even for a second.

As I got to the front door, I told him he looked handsome, and all I got in return was a polite smile as he shut the door behind me. He didn't tell me I looked beautiful, he didn't tell me I looked nice, he couldn't even manage a "you too." I sat in the car and was straight on my phone in a huff but again, it was soon forgotten when we got to the restaurant and had to play happy families.

That night was up there with one of the shittiest I had ever felt about Chris and me. Back home and in bed, he tried to come on to me as I was seconds away from falling asleep. "We had it last night, Chris, " I told him, as I was absolutely exhausted.

"But I won't see you for three weeks, " he said.

"Chris, I'm shattered, and I've got a lot to do and sort tomorrow morning. Please just let me sleep." I didn't back down. The week had utterly taken it out of me: I was stressed, anxiety-riddled – I'd had even had a panic attack five days prior. I physically didn't have the energy.

Chris rolled over so his back was facing me, without a single care in the world. No kiss, no goodnight, not another sound, and he went to sleep.

The next morning, it was as if the last few days hadn't even happened. He took Noah out early so I could finish packing. As the pair of them walked through the door when they returned, I was walking down the stairs and heard, "Mummy, presents!"

I sat down on the bottom step and opened each and every gift. Chris then gave me an envelope and told me there was a letter inside for every day I was on the mountain. There was also another envelope full of messages from my loved ones to read on the plane. I couldn't see straight from the tears. I suddenly felt guilty about the night before and thought, *here he is, this is the man I love.*

The first thing I did every morning when I was on the mountain was read Chris's letters. They helped me to get through the day, helped me to keep going and not give up. They were beautiful. But other than those letters, I didn't really think of him a lot. I didn't miss him. I don't know if it was because each day I was just so occupied by literally staying alive, I don't know. Perhaps it was because I hadn't felt independent for such a long time. I didn't do anything on my own. It was rare to be without him or Noah, so I felt free.

Despite everything I was feeling, all my confessions to Amy about not missing Chris, I still couldn't wait to hear from him. I wanted to think everything I was feeling was just a minor blip, and talking to him or reading his messages would settle all my wandering thoughts. But when I checked my phone back at the hotel after our descent, the only person that hadn't messaged me was Chris. There I was, like a ghost, ignoring all the other heartfelt messages I'd received and trying to find his name, but it was nowhere to be seen. So, I texted him:

Baby, I made it. I'm back at the hotel.

Well done. ♥

How come I didn't have a text waiting for me?

Well, I knew you wouldn't get them.

The triumphant smile was wiped off my face within seconds. I felt like the one person who I wanted to boast and gloat to, the person I thought would burst with proudness, didn't care at all. I went from being on top of the world (quite literally) to feeling so inferior. But the thing that kept me going was knowing Chris would be at the airport. I knew I would know how I truly felt when I saw him. He was staying at my parents' house the night before so that he could leave Noah in bed while he and Dad drove to the airport. Without Noah being there, there was nothing to cloud my judgement. It would just be him and me.

And then he didn't fucking get up.

My heart felt like it was shattering into tiny pieces. Sobbing my heart out to my dad the entire journey home, I still clung to hope; clung on to the man I had known for eleven years, convincing myself he wouldn't do this to me. My heart wouldn't let go without one more tiny fight. Maybe he didn't show up because he'd planned something special for when I walked through the door…

That tiny bit of hope vanished in the glint of a second.

He didn't get off the fucking sofa.

And I knew in that exact moment our relationship was over.

You've got to learn to leave the table when love is no longer being served.

~Nina Simone

I won't share the to-and-fro motions that followed, but I will confess that I broke up with the love of my life, the father of my child, my fiancé, via text. I regret this so much, and probably will for the rest of my life, but I knew if I saw him, if I saw all the hurt in his eyes, I wouldn't be able to walk away. He spent days pleading with me that he knew he'd fucked up, begging me for another chance. But I couldn't give in. It felt like reading a book I'd read before. I knew exactly how it was going to end.

I know deep down that breaking up was the right thing to do, but that doesn't take away from the fact that it was the hardest thing I have ever done. People say it is harder to break someone else's heart than have your own broken. Why? Because if you get your heart broken, there is absolutely nothing you can do about it. Nothing will persuade the other person to stay with you. But when the ball is in your court, you never know if you're making the biggest mistake of your life. You just have to go with your gut instinct and how you're feeling at the time and hope that in the long run, it was the right decision. But you will never know if it is. You will never know how your life would have panned out if you stayed.

Initially, many of my friends said, "There is no fairy tale, Elle. Every relationship gets boring after a while." And that's when the doubt started to kick in: did the spark go because I let it? Did it go because I didn't try and fix it? Did I give up too easily? Was it my fault? Maybe I should have walked up to him the second he walked through the door. Maybe I should have offered him more massages after long days at work instead of expecting them. When you're out of a situation, you forget so quickly how it made you feel and the doubt plays on your mind daily. Was I really that unhappy? Surely it wasn't that bad? Maybe I have commitment issues? What if I always think there is someone out there that is better for me? Or someone else that will treat me better or love me more? What if I just always want more? What if I'm the problem?

I didn't just lose my partner; I also lost my best friend. I lost two people in one, and that itself is heartache like no other. We grew up together, so I lost a whole family too; people that I saw as my own brothers and sisters. I can't count on my hands how many friends I also lost. It's not like taking a knife. It's like taking ten, all in your back. I received abusive messages from some of his friends, and even some of my closest friends distanced themselves from me because they didn't agree with what I'd done. People will never understand how you feel and know the ins and outs of a relationship; they will just leave you out in the cold all by yourself.

I didn't end it with Chris because I wanted someone else. I didn't want anyone else but him, but I felt starved of love. When you choose to be with someone, they aren't just your lover and your best friend; they are also your partner in crime, your help, your protector. You are committed to each other.

Even so, there isn't a day that goes by that I don't think about him with nostalgia racing through my veins. I miss him. I miss him so much. I miss the way he used to make me laugh. I miss the way I couldn't stay mad at him because he would tickle me or tell a silly joke. I miss the smell of his hair and his perfect lips and green eyes. I miss the way he stroked my hair off my face again and again, but then I would get mad because he was making it greasy. I miss him telling me to stop biting my lip before he knew I was going to cry. I miss telling him every little thing that happened to me that day. I miss being a family. I miss my best friend. I think I will miss those things forever.

I'm learning how to miss someone without wanting them back.

~Faraway

I constantly have this gut-wrenching feeling that I wasted so much of his time, that I wasted so much of his life. He is the only person where I really think I wasted their time. I've stolen so much from him. He is such a family person; he could have been happily married with three kids by now, but he's not because of me. I know he wouldn't think like that because we have Noah, but I feel overwhelmed with guilt. It hurts me so much that I could do that to another human. I wasn't breaking up with him because I had fallen out of love with him, that wasn't the case at all. I was doing it for myself, I wasn't going to settle for this mediocre life. Love had taken on a different meaning for me. My mind was made up. I had to leave for good this time.

I left because I deserved better, not because I didn't love him.

~Tabs

Now, when he comes and picks Noah up for the weekend, I try my best to make conversation, to ask how he is, to ask about work, to ask what their plans together are, but he just stands there. I ask because I want Noah to see that his parents can have a healthy relationship and be in the same room together but also because I care about Chris. I always will. I don't ever want him to be hurt again the way I hurt him. I hope that one day he can look me in the eyes. I hope that one day, he will forgive me. I think that the reason why I kept doing what I did – not wanting him but not wanting anyone else to have him either – is because he is the only person who has ever told me they loved me. If he loved someone else, who would be left to love me? And I realise that's so unfair. I don't know how I will feel this time around when Chris moves on, but I know I see things very differently now. I want him to move on. I want him to be happy.

I think we were meant to be, just not forever. We were supposed to bring the most beautiful little boy in the world, but that is where our story ends. It wasn't until I was writing the last chapter of this book that I knew. Despite everything that happened after the split (which you'll learn about as you read on), I still didn't want to run back to him. There is not a bone in my body that ever felt the need to text him – drunk text him even – or to go back. That's when I knew I made the right decision.

There is a very thin line between liking someone romantically and caring for them as a friend.

Chapter Three
The Mountain – Continued

She was life itself. Wild and free. Wonderfully chaotic. A perfectly put together mess.

~The Better Man Project

A month after we got back from the climb, the four of us planned a night out together. After splitting up with Chris, I just needed a night out with good company. Jack and Reece met us at the hotel where Amy and I were staying, not far from where they both lived. As we danced away in our room, drinking champagne and getting our glad rags on, the men waited for us in the lobby. When the doors of the elevator opened, their faces were a picture. We weren't the women they knew from the mountain – we were inside, but on the outside, they had never seen us like this! Hair done, makeup on, dressed to kill. Their faces quickly turned to panic, worried they were underdressed. Jack wearing khaki tracksuit bottoms, and Reece wearing baggy cotton shorts, both with Nike trainers. We couldn't have looked more opposite to them if we tried.

Off we trailed around Liverpool city centre, getting rejected by all of the bars because the guys were dressed too casually. After walking for what felt like hours in the wet and cold, we settled for the only place that would let us in, TGI Fridays. *Classy*. But we didn't care where we were – that's the thing about good company, you could be anywhere in the world, it doesn't matter. It was like nothing had changed, that we were back in our little bubble, the four of us together: laughing and joking, reminiscing about our times on the mountain, chatting about Amy and her boyfriend, Jack and his girlfriend, Reece's work, and my not-so-happy story of the separation from Chris. In just four weeks of not seeing each other so much had happened, so much to talk about. The more we talked, the more the drinks were flowing – too quickly for me, and things got very blurry. Jack and his girlfriend were leaving for Milan in the early hours, so we decided to have a nightcap at our hotel before they left. This was the first night that I had turned to alcohol to try and escape how I was feeling.

There is a thin line between liking someone romantically and caring for them as a friend. I embarrassingly put this to the test. My feet were blistering from the new strappy heels I'd bought for the occasion, so I went back to the hotel room to change them. Jack accompanied me in my drunken state – stumbling in and out of the elevator, struggling to get the key card to fit the door, before helping me out of my stupid-ass heels. I was a mess, but unfortunately, it didn't stop there. Within minutes of being in the room, I flung myself onto the bed and tried to pull Jack on top of me. I grabbed the back of his neck and pulled him even closer to me. I went in for the kill – the big kiss.

He pulled away. Frustrated and enraged, he left me sprawled out on the bed and shouted, "I can't do this, I have a girlfriend. Why would you do that? We're friends, Elle!"

Rejection shot through me like an electric shock, and I instantly started to cry. What had I done? Had I just ruined our friendship in a flicker of a second? Never mind the disrespect of knowing he had a girlfriend. I hadn't felt rejected in years; I'm absolutely terrified of it, and the tears quickly turned into anger. "Fuck off to Milan then, go and be with your girlfriend!" I shouted back. *What was I doing?* He was furious and said he needed to leave. I quickly switched again, trying to reason with him and begging him to stay, coming off as a drunken, desperate mess, but he was having none of it.

I stumbled back out the door, attempting to put on my slip-on Vans, one shoe on my foot and the other in my hand. I made it to the elevator but as the doors opened we both slumped against opposite sides in silence; it was like we were strangers. We walked straight over to Amy and Reece, and they intuitively knew something had happened. "What's up with you two?" Amy nervously asked.

"Nothing, he's leaving!" I sniggered. "Bye Jack." Within twenty seconds he went, leaving the hotel.

Trying to drown my sorrows of embarrassment and rejection, Amy and I talked over more drinks. "He does have a girlfriend, though, babe. You shouldn't have stuck it on him. Why would you want to ruin your friendship?"

She was entirely right, and even though she tried to console me, the tears wouldn't stop. I had all this heartbreak that I still hadn't dealt with and a very hazy head. I stupidly thought there was more to it with Jack; that deep down maybe he was the reason I'd split up with Chris. I was so desperate to feel wanted that I took my chance, not thinking about the bigger picture, that I could ruin not just one friendship but the most precious friendship – the one between the four of us.

The rest of the night was pretty much a blur, and I woke up to all sorts of bruises and cuts. But nothing hurt more in the morning than the sheer anxiety and embarrassment I felt about what had happened the night before.

You'll never be able to drink the sadness or anxiety away. The only thing you'll be drinking away is your sanity.

~Unknown

Jack and I didn't speak for weeks afterwards. I was too embarrassed to reach out to him, to apologise. It was only when I decided to go back to Liverpool to see my brother and his girlfriend that I put my big girl pants on and asked to meet up with him and Reece. "Of course, " he said, and suggested a local pub.

I felt so nervous about seeing him. What if he was different now? What if he saw me in a different light? What if he was going to give me a good taste of my own medicine and shout at me? But this is Jack we are talking about. Deep down, I knew he would never do any of those things, and I was correct.

The second I saw him, he picked me up, squeezed me and kissed me on my forehead like a long-lost friend. We ate dinner, had a couple of drinks and joked about me being rejected by him. We laughed it off as he told me not to worry about it, but I made sure he knew it would never happen again.

That's when I realised what a true friend was. Someone who would always love you – the imperfect you, the confused you, the wrong you – because that is what people are supposed to do.

~R.J.L.

Since then, I've seen Jack countless times. He's like a comfort blanket now. Not a week goes by without talking to him. Whenever I am down, he sings until I've cheered up or refuses to put down the phone until I feel better. He is still with his girlfriend, but regardless of whether he is or not, this would never change things. I am so thankful for our friendship. I would never want to ruin what we have. Never mind the embarrassment of getting rejected again! But it really is not like that with us. I have spoken to him about every guy I've been seeing, and nine times out of ten, he is always right about what type of man they are and how it's going to end. He is so caring and protective that I would never ever want him out of my life. He is one of only a couple of the men in this book whose chapter will never be closed. He is a massive part of my life and one of the best men I am fortunate to call a friend, and I never want that to change.

That is why I feel pain so deeply, because I remember all the bad things people have said to me. I can't let them go.

Chapter Four
The Doubt

"But people are oceans," she shrugged. "You cannot know them by their surface."

~Beau Taplin

I am easily defined by the people that know me well, but to the people that don't, I am not anything like they think I am. My friends and family would describe me as insecure and sensitive. You wouldn't believe that if you saw me on a night out or you were one of my ten thousand followers on Instagram, but you would if you knew how many shots it took to get that one picture I uploaded because I hated myself in the other eighty-seven. Because it's all a front. I post photos to make myself feel better, for gratification, to see the likes and the comments. It's pathetic, I know. From the way I portray myself on social media, you might not believe that I have insecurities. But I do. We all do.

I had a breast augmentation at twenty-two as I was as flat as a pancake. The boys at school used to walk past me and make an ironing board motion *(boys are only mean to you if they like you – yeah, right)*. All my life, I've wanted to change my face. If I'd had the money, I would have had a lot of plastic surgery by now, and I can't even blame social media for that. Of course, it made it a hundred times worse, but even when I was in my teens, before the days of Instagram, I used to dread the yearbook photos or the group school photo coming out because of how I looked and that everyone else would be able to see it.

On the flip side, I get a lot of compliments, although I rarely accept them. The second I say, "Thank you" or agree, I worry

I will be seen as up myself or arrogant. You know, the Regina George, "Oh so you agree? You think you're pretty?" moment on *Mean Girls*? I can't stand the thought of people thinking I am rude, so over the years I've become overfriendly. I reply to every person that texts me or messages and comments on my Instagram because the thought of people thinking I think I am better than them makes my skin crawl. I know I'm not. I care far too much what people think about me, and it's exhausting.

Some girls say they're not pretty because they know someone's gonna come and say, "Shut up, you know you are." But some girls say they're not pretty, not because they're looking for attention but because that's how they feel.

~Unknown

I have always suffered from social anxiety. Sometimes I throw up at the thought of walking into a bar and worrying about what people will think and say about me. And OK, you might say, "Well, don't wear provocative things or get tattoos, and you might not get looked at and talked about as much." But the way I dress and my tattoos have always been part of my creativity and how I express myself. In every job interview and every school report, I was described as the bubbliest, chattiest, happiest person. Yet walking into a group situation, I cower away and stay quiet until I feel comfortable. I am a walking contradiction.

My whole life, I've been told: "Stop taking everything to heart, stop being so sensitive." For years it has been drilled into me that being sensitive is a bad thing and a sign of weakness. I take everything to heart – every insult, every critique, all feedback, comments, reports, everything – and in every aspect of my life I have always struggled to accept even positive criticism, be it in school, at work, or even when playing sports that I love. Some people thrive on constructive feedback; it makes them work harder, whereas it has the opposite effect on me. It pushes me into a more negative mindset, and I start overthinking.

At school, I got straight As in physical and creative subjects – physical education, art, textiles and English. If it didn't keep my mind busy, I was bored and easily distracted. When I got to university, I failed most of my presentations because I would get nervous and my mind couldn't focus. But written projects, I would pass with flying colours because I was invested. That's why I love books – I get sucked straight in as if I'm living what they are going through. I have never been very good at telling stories. If I had a pound for every time someone said: "We haven't got all day, Elle" or "Come on, spit it out!" I would be living in the Bahamas right now. Christ, I can't even tell a joke. I forget things and get everything muddled up because my mind is always elsewhere. Thinking about something else, thinking about other people, thinking about aliens or the world ending, my mind just never rests. It is full of so much beauty and yet so much darkness.

That's why I write. Because when I do, no one interrupts me, no one tells me to spit my words out or hurry up with my story, and no one tells me that's not how the story went. The words that I can't seem to get out before I get all tongue-tied naturally come out clearly on paper. People say writers are forgetful but they remember everything, and that could not be truer when it comes to me. I will forget what you had for lunch, but I will remember the exact shade of colour of every piece of clothing you were wearing. I will forget your pet's name, but I will remember exactly how you smelt. They say writers are forgetful because they're busy remembering all the important things. That is why I feel pain so deeply, because I remember all the bad things people have said to me. I can't let it go.

I remember at school when my cross-country picture was on the wall because I won a race, and someone wrote *SLUT* on it. I was thirteen years old. I will never forget that. I just cannot forget things, and that is why I find it so hard to forget the people that walk out of my life and all that was said in between.

The most dangerous heart disease: strong memory.

~Nizar Qabbani

I say sorry a lot. It's a very British thing, but another thing that has been drilled into me my whole life: "Stop saying sorry all the time." It comes as natural to me as saying hello or goodbye. If someone opens the door for me, I say sorry before I say thank you. If someone goes for the same item as me in a shop, I say sorry and let them have it. For most things that are not my fault in day-to-day life, like brushing past someone, I will apologise. In everyday situations, like wanting a drink from a friend's house, I will apologise. However, catch me in an argument, and I will damn right not apologise. I'm a stubborn little shit. Again, a walking contradiction.

On the other hand, my friends and family would describe me as caring, loving and kind. I would literally do anything for anyone. I would drop anything in the world if someone were hurt or upset. I've made myself ill in the past because I have never learnt how to say no. I say yes to everyone and everything because I can't bear the thought of letting others down. So, I run around most days like a bat out of hell trying to please everyone. I won't turn work down because I can't stand the thought of someone going elsewhere; even if the timeframe is unrealistic I put so much pressure on myself to make it happen. I burn the candle at both ends. Always.

I feel powerful emotions. When I am up, I'm sky high. I become impulsive and as if nothing can stop me. But when I am down, I feel like I'm drowning, and nothing can save me. I notice the slightest shift in someone's mood and continually ask other people if they're OK if I have done something to upset them, worrying and overthinking that I might have hurt their feelings somehow. I am just an all or nothing kind of woman. I either starve myself or overeat; fall madly in love or hate passionately; turn a programme off after two minutes or watch the whole series in one go; have sober nights or get blind drunk. I don't know what balance is, I never have.

I don't know what living a balanced life feels like.
When I am sad, I don't cry; I pour.
When I am happy, I don't smile I glow.
When I am angry, I don't yell I burn.

The good thing about feeling in extremes is,
When I love, I give them wings,
But perhaps that isn't
Such a good thing cause

They always tend to leave.
And you should see me,
When my heart is broken,
I don't grieve,
I shatter.

~Rupi Kaur

Then I became a mum, and my insecurities got worse. I was never really bothered about my body changing when I was pregnant. I had a well-earnt six-pack when I fell pregnant, and all I wanted was a bump. Every day I woke up excited to see if it popped out. I drank so much water that it bloated me so it looked like I had a bump. Even though there was a chance of getting stretch marks, I accepted it: *If I get them, I get them.* I was having a baby with someone I loved; someone who also loved me and my body and this baby. I wasn't bothered if we had a takeaway four nights in a row and were getting fatter by the day. Because I had him, and at the time, I thought I was going to be with him forever.

Then came Noah's birth. I am such an active person, and I was desperate to avoid a C-section. The thought of the aftercare, all the potential health problems afterwards, never mind during, and let's not even mention the scar. The second they told me I had to have an emergency C-section, I burst into floods of tears. Chris couldn't even look at me as he knew how desperate I was to avoid it. But I had to suck it up for the sake of my son's life. It wasn't about me right there and then; it was about him and his safety.

After three days in the hospital, we came home. Within a day we were already off to the pub garden, enjoying the amazing May sunshine. Then within two weeks of being home, I woke up to what looked like a scene from Dexter. Blood and pus covered the bed, and my scar had split open at both ends. I had been pretending I was OK and of course, typical me, I hadn't listened to the professionals. I had been doing everything they told me not to. It was gruesome, and it wasn't until that morning that I thought: *Shit, have I fucked up this scar? What the hell is it going to look like now?*

If you have had a C-section, you will know that most women have a bloated tummy for some time afterwards. After about six weeks I remember my tummy going down, but it had turned to jelly. I still wasn't allowed to do any form of exercise for another two months, and it hit me like a tonne of bricks. The kangaroo pouch that people talk about after having a caesarean is real. Those first few months, I would lie in bed wide awake thinking. *What if I can never get rid of it?* One night I was up until five o'clock. I know having a new-born can cause sleep deprivation, but this night wasn't down to that. I sat up for maybe seven hours and Googled C-section scars and kangaroo pouches. I then went on to searching through the Instagram models that had had caesareans and how unreal their bodies looked straight after birth. I was a wreck. Most of what I read online said you will have the layer of skin or pouch forever, and it is highly unlikely you will ever get rid of it. Well, that set me off scrolling from website to website, reading about getting liposuction to get rid of this awful pouch. I wasn't even thinking about the fact that the most precious thing in my life had just come out from there. I just couldn't shake the fact that my body was never ever going to be the same again.

The more I dwelled on it, the more down I became, and my comfort eating was getting out of control, making me feel lazier than ever. I started to think I had a case of the baby blues, but I knew I was just stuck in a rut that felt hard to get out of. My new season of netball trials was approaching, and for the first time ever I thought, *Jesus Elle, you are a lazy couch potato. You are never going to get on the team this year.* So, one morning, I decided enough was enough. It was time to stop feeling sorry for myself and get my ass into gear by going back to the gym. The more I exercised, the more it became my get away from parenthood, even if it was just for an hour a day. My competitive side came rushing back when I set myself goals and knew I had to earn my place back in the netball squad, and five months later, I had shed all my pregnancy weight and looked almost as good as I ever did. I didn't have lipo, and I began to love my scar and the slight pouch I knew I could never get rid of. I did it for me, not for my fiancé or anyone else, but to make sure I didn't lose that little bit of me and to feel good about myself.

Unfortunately, fast-forward to singledom, the insecurities came rushing back. I found myself at an all-time low. I started to notice all the little things that I'd previously overlooked because I knew Chris was in awe of my body. After all, it had brought his child into this world. I noticed how my breasts had stretch marks from going from a D to an F cup when my milk came in; from them being perky and round to droopier and needing to go back to wearing bras. Every night I would look at the stretch marks on my inner thighs from where I put on three and a half stone. I was my own worst enemy, becoming obsessed with my flaws.

Why are you so unkind to me?

My body cries.

Cause you don't look like them,

I tell her.

~Rupi Kaur

So, there I was, single and genuinely wondering if I'd ever have sex again; whether I could be naked in front of another man with all these scars and marks. *If I sleep with someone, do I tell them that I had a C-section and that I have a huge scar across my stomach?* In reality, all they want in that split second is sex, and I'm positive it's a mood killer if I've ever heard one before. I know deep down that it is the most beautiful scar in the world because it is how my son was brought into the world, but I was now petrified about how men would see it. Would they see it as off-putting or ugly? Again, I was crushing my mind with how other people would see me and think of me.

With all these materialistic insecurities swarming around my head, it wasn't long until the self-doubt about never finding love again kicked in. My closest friends would describe me as a hopeless romantic. They say, "Elle loves to love, " and it couldn't be more accurate: I love "love" – the idea of it, the feeling of it, everything. I am such a romantic. I feel like I was born in the wrong era. I want to bump into the love of my life at a coffee house or bookstore, not swipe right on Tinder. I want to dance under the stars in the streets, not grind on someone in a nightclub. I want love letters posted to my house, not a notification because someone is sliding into my direct messages on Instagram.

I'm just too in love with love for anything less than that heart racing, soul craving, lose my breath, and feel my infinity in the beating of your chest, kind of love.

~Butterflies Rising

So, this brings me to dating apps. To be honest with you, they just cringe me out – the whole bio thing, for starters.

Elle, 28, hairdresser

Wants children but already has one.

Wants to get married eventually but so far, one engagement down.

It isn't exactly a selling point, is it? And then you have to choose your best five photos, cringe. Do I put bikini pictures up? Do I put old pictures up where I look my skinniest and most youthful? Do I put a picture of Noah and me up? It's all just so forced. That's why, deep down, I don't think the dating app thing is for me, because it's down to looks. You swipe right if you like the look of someone, then if it is a match, you start talking, and after two weeks, you realise you've wasted your time because the beautiful face doesn't match the personality. I need a connection. Of course, I am not going to lie, I'm obviously attracted to good looking guys, but there's just got to be so much more than that. Looks fade, so when you are eighty, sitting next to the love of your life in your rocking chair, you want to still be in love because of the way they make you feel; the way they make you laugh until your wrinkly jelly belly hurts. Not because they looked like Prince Charming fifty years before. I'm attracted to personality; I always have been.

You can laugh me into bed.

~Unknown

So, should I swipe right to every single guy who isn't strikingly good looking on the off chance they might have a fantastic personality, and I'll have a connection with them? No, I'm a working mum remember, I don't have time for that, and I think a connection is rare to find these days – for me, anyway. So, then, what am I waiting for? The love of my life to accidentally choose my house to burgle? Or maybe it's the DPD driver that is always happy to see me. Perhaps I should invite him in for a tea or coffee and see if we have a connection? Too desperate? Yeah, thought so.

My point is, there can't just be one person in this world for us. I think you'd be lucky these days to fall in love with someone in your teens and be with them for the rest of your life. But it just isn't how our generation works anymore; there are too many options out there – dating apps, social media, women that throw themselves at married guys on nights out, guys that throw themselves at married women on nights out. I just wish I lived a hundred years ago when there really was "the one", and nothing got in the way of that.

It started to hit me, the daunting idea that no one will want someone who was previously engaged-to-be-married and has a child. "Baggage", you might call it. I am not naïve. I know a man's first choice wouldn't be to find a woman who already has a child with another man. I know it, they know it – the whole world knows it. It's like taking a punch in the stomach, imagining someone wouldn't want to be with me because I have a child. I am so proud to be a mother, it is undoubtedly the best thing in the world, and I wouldn't change it for anything. Of course, I wouldn't want to be with a jackass who rejected me because I have a child anyway, but many men don't realise that until they are in too deep. That's what scares me.

They wouldn't just be leaving me; they would be leaving Noah too. Leaving the best thing that ever happened to me. The thought of that hurt trumps all the pain I've ever felt, and I think about it all the time.

There's also the question of when is the right time to tell someone you have a child? In some respects, this is why I think it's easier to meet people through social media or mutual friends because you don't have to have that awkward conversation telling them you have a child and seeing their face drop right in front of your eyes. You can practically see the cogs working in their brain as they start thinking: *Oh, I don't want to be a stepdad, that's not for me.* I get it, I'm not stupid; it's not what men aspire to be in life. But when you meet someone on a night out, for example, at what point do you slip into conversation that you're a mum?

"Would you like a drink?"

"Oh yes, I'd love one, please, make it a double vodka and soda. And by the way, I have a two-year-old at home."

You can't do right from wrong. If you tell them, they may think, *Christ, why is she telling me she's got a child? I only want a one-night stand. I'm not going to marry her.* If you don't tell them, end up taking them back to your place and they trip over a toy train, they think you're a psycho for luring them back to yours without giving them the heads up. It's all very confusing and very easy to overthink – especially when you're like me.

Our greatest battles are those with our own minds.

~Jameson Frank

It was crazy to think only two years ago, I wanted to be with the same man for the rest of my life and have maybe three or four children with him. I never wanted Noah to be an only child, I never wanted him to grow up without siblings, I never

ever wanted to be someone that had children from more than one man, ever. That unnerved me in so many ways. I come from an unbroken home, where my parents are still pretty much head over heels for each other, with an older brother who I am incredibly close to, so I have nothing to compare to apart from a happy, loving family. I know it's becoming more and more normalised these days to have children with different fathers, but I can't help but think what happens if the second relationship doesn't work out? You are single again, with two children, both from different men. Do you try again? Do you have three children by three different dads? Three different surnames, three different drop-offs to each child's father (if they want to be involved, that is). I don't know if I could go through that again.

That's me, always thinking about what my future might hold. It feels so blurry; the uncertainty scares me to death. It's almost terrifying to think, is that it? Have I had my one chance at love, and nothing good will come my way again? Am I not going to have any more children? I see all these women with children from previous relationships that are now happier than ever in new ones, pregnant or engaged, but I can't help thinking that it's not on the cards for me, that it's just not going to happen to me again in this lifetime.

It was friends with benefits. But we all know that can go one way or the other.

Chapter Five
The Rebound

Sex: the thing that takes up the least amount of time and causes the most amount of trouble.

~John Barrymore

Everyone knows a guy that you could message for sex, right? A bit of fun, no strings attached kind of thing. Well, this is all that I needed, and I didn't care if it happened once or fifty times, as long as it took my mind off what I was going through. I just needed to feel wanted, but it ended up having the opposite effect.

Aaron was tall, dark and handsome, but when I say Aaron is tall, I mean he's over six foot six tall and built like a brick shit house. He was a well-known ladies man, so I knew I wouldn't have a problem with being rejected because, quite frankly, I think he sleeps with anything with a heartbeat. We'd had a one-night stand together around six years ago when Chris and I split up for the second time. I remember being on the same page with him when it came to sex. I have always been open-minded and experimental when it comes to the bedroom, and over the years, I quickly realised what I enjoyed wasn't everyone's cup of tea.

I have never had a problem with talking about sex, I have never seen it as a taboo subject. However maybe my level of 'sex talk' is a taboo subject in itself. No details are ever left untouched when unfolding explicit details of nights of passion to my friends. Hell, there's been many a time my friends have been left gaping like a fish or covering their ears but for me, it's just natural. But I knew he could give me what I wanted, so not long into being single, I reached out to him by sending a reaction to one of his Instagram stories (*how subtle of me*). Within minutes, he replied: "Guessing you're back on the market then?"

We only sent a couple of messages to one another before he laid his cards on the table. "If you need a little rebound, you know where I am!"

Bingo!

We joked about how unfortunate it was that we had only slept with each other once all those years ago, and he teased: "Well, my schedule is clear for a refresher course."

I don't know what came over me, but I didn't seem to give a fuck what he thought and replied, "Tomorrow night too soon?"

"Works for me, trouble." Aaron was exactly how I remembered.

Looking back through our messages, it's clear what happened was inevitable. We talked about why we both decided to be single, and he was quick to ask if his ex and I were friends because that would be too close to home. I mean, the empathy was there, I'll give him that. I explained that we knew each other, but we weren't so-called friends, and this wasn't the first time our paths had crossed when it came to men.

We carried on talking for the rest of the night – just chitchat, catching up about where we both were with life and work. "I'm not as bad as I used to be…" he said. I remember thinking, *Maybe I've got him all wrong. Perhaps he's not the playboy he was six years ago. He might have calmed down.* But that's me, always giving people the benefit of the doubt, believing their every word and trying to see the best in them.

The conversation later turned to heartbreak, with us both admitting we were heartbreakers from our previous relationships. "I don't think there's a heart in here. That's my problem, " he said.

I don't think that's the case, though. Aaron has had quite a few relationships, so I think he must understand what it's like to fall for someone. Granted, they never seem to last that long, and knowing what I know now, it's quite simple to see why.

It was getting late, and we were both in bed. "The quicker you go to sleep, the quicker you'll get a roll around tomorrow, " he said, bold as brass. It still shocks me that you can get sex on tap if you want to these days, but just like that, I could, and my plan had worked.

The following day he messaged to ask what time I was coming over. He really was quite the charmer, asking if I would need feeding before we got down to it. I had to sink a quick glass of prosecco before I left, to let the bubbles go to my head, to try and help calm my nerves. As he answered the door, "Long time no see, hey?" came blurting out of my mouth as we hugged, but I think we were both nervous. It had been such a long time since we last saw each other, and it can be so awkward when you have arranged to literally just have sex with someone.

Luckily the conversation never got boring as we sat around his kitchen and barely looked at our phones the whole night. He was funny – *really funny* – and my God, he smelt so good. I would have had him there and then in the kitchen if he came on to me, but I was so sheepish and so nervous, like I couldn't remember how to have sex. I never would have come onto him first. I wouldn't have known how to.

I suppose it's weird to be with the same person for five years and then suddenly have someone else see your naked body, someone else feeling you, kissing you. Mostly my different, post-baby body, might I add. I was massively overthinking it, but I couldn't ease my mind from spinning, and I don't think the beers were helping either.

Fuck me deeper than my thoughts go.

~Liv Armelle

After hours of chatter, polishing off thirteen beers between us, he said he needed to go to bed as he had work in the morning. It was as if he gave me the eyes, like a signal, and it was a race to the bedroom. Already panting after running two flights of stairs of his three-storey, posh terrace house, we both ripped off our clothes, and the red lace underwear that I so carefully picked out was tossed on the floor. Grabbing one another's face, kissing passionately, I fell on the bed, and within seconds he had spread my legs and started to go down on me. Memories came flooding back at how good he was with his tongue; I could have lain there for hours. I think he would have too. His large hands grabbed my waist and flipped me over, my back arched, and the side of my face pressed into his soft, cream sheets as he entered me. I had forgotten how big he was. He was so rough as if he knew I needed it like that, slapping my arse with every thrust as I moaned louder and louder in the same rhythm. He flipped me back over like I didn't have a choice in the position and propped me on his waist. Slowly rolling my hips back and forth, up and down, getting used to his size, we both let out aggressive moans. The alcohol intake made it last an exceptionally long time. Dripping with sweat, we went in every position, throwing my legs above my head as he got deeper and deeper. It went on and on. I didn't have a single care in the world – other than the satisfaction I was receiving. Actually, my only care was how sore I would be in the morning.

He took a shower and got back into bed, and we were both asleep within minutes. In the morning, both with slightly fuzzy heads, he made us a cup of tea and then I made my way over to the front door to leave. There was no goodbye kiss or anything, just a hug and me pretending to be all innocent, thanking him for having me (quite literally) before we went our separate ways, saying we would see each other soon.

Later that day, after returning from work, I received a picture message of a lipstick, a pair of earrings and a diamond ring. "You left these here. You'll have to come round soon and collect them."

This is where it gets awkward. The lipstick and the earrings were mine, but not the diamond ring. Little did he know I'd seen the ring on the bedside table before we went to sleep. "Well, I will definitely come and collect my belongings soon – not the ring though, as it isn't mine!" He was quick to defend himself, insisting that it had to be mine, and if it wasn't, he didn't know whose it was. He even claimed that he wasn't sleeping with anyone else and that he was "basically celibate these days", that the ring must have been the cleaner's *(I mean, I know I'm blonde but come on).* I wasn't really bothered if he was sleeping with anyone else, but if he was, I would have removed myself from the situation and not gone back for more. It gets so messy otherwise, but silly old me chose to believe him.

I decided to lighten the mood and show him a picture of the bright red bruises he had left me with. "Well, you definitely left your mark on me, boy." He was delighted with himself, so I shot him straight down and told him I wanted him to bruise me more, hit me harder, choke me harder. He promised he would, and he didn't disappoint.

Choke me, she whispered, empty me of all the air and fill me with you.

~Akif Kichloo

One evening I was out for drinks with a couple of friends, and his name popped up on my phone. With the bright light, it wasn't hard for my friends to glance over and see the name. "You're not sleeping with Aaron, are you?" As I nervously laughed, they were quick to warn me: "Just be careful, Elle, don't get in too deep with him."

I enjoyed the time I spent with Aaron, but I kept the line fully marked on the floor. Contact when we weren't together was minimal. We'd exchange the odd text asking how the other one was or how their day had been, and maybe a few jokes or pictures here and there. Other than that, it was pretty much "When are you next free?" Or "Have you got kiddo tonight? If not, are you coming over?" It was friends with benefits. But we all know that can go one way or the other.

Each time I went over to his, it got earlier and earlier, and each time the sex got rougher and rougher. The hair pulling got harder (*I don't know how my extensions made it*), and the choking got tighter. He gave me exactly what I asked from him except once when I asked him to do it even harder, to push the limit, and he proceeded to choke me to the point where I thought I would pass out (I think my neck was on the line at that point). "I can't breathe, not quite that hard, Jesus, " I joked, although I felt like I was actually praying to Jesus as I was fighting for my last dying breath, but it was part of the thrill and just the way I liked it. One thing I liked about Aaron, though, was that he was very giving. Each time we had sex, he would always go down on me first and wouldn't finish until he made me squirt at least three times. He once made me explode five times in a row with me, screaming, "Fuck! How can you do that to me? How can you be that good?" Just giving him the extra ego boost that he definitely didn't need or deserve. I didn't even think I had that much fluid inside me, but my God, he knew what he was doing. He must have a degree in fingering women.

Aaron also had a mirror perfectly positioned facing the bed and loved to watch himself fuck. I mean, I am all for that. I love to watch myself in a mirror too, but oh, how Aaron liked to watch what he was doing. Every time we had sex, we would squabble about the lights being on or off. I have always been extremely confident during sex but having a child, having my scar on show in plain sight to someone that wasn't the father, just knocked my confidence for six, and I couldn't imagine having sex with someone in broad daylight ever again. But he did make me feel good, he did make me feel like I had nothing to worry about, so we agreed that it would be medium lighting. Not lights on, not lights off, but dimmed, enough to see each other (or for him to see himself, shall I say).

Each time we had sex, there was no cuddling afterwards, a small dose of legs intertwined watching TV but no real form of affection whatsoever, which I usually would want but not with Aaron. I was there for one reason and one reason only. However, I did really like him as a friend. He made me laugh, he was kind and thoughtful, he even defrosted my car for me one morning. *What a gent!* But it was exactly what I needed. When I was there, I wasn't a mum, I wasn't heartbroken, and I wasn't sad. I was just me, enjoying his company and having some great sex. He seemed to really let his guard down with me, and we had deep conversations about his family, how he wanted a family of his own one day and about my life with Noah. Stripped back from his ego and his promiscuous ways, he had a heart of gold and the potential to make a woman incredibly happy.

We are in bed laughing, and we don't care about anything.

~Charles Bukowski

As the weeks went on, I started to feel confident again and extremely comfortable around him. The last time I saw him I went over at four o'clock in the afternoon, and within two minutes of being in his house, our clothes were off and we were having sex in broad daylight. We then shared a Chinese takeaway and watched TV shows all night together. I began to think, I can do this friend with benefits thing. I've been burned with this situation before (we'll get to him later), so I felt like I had learnt my lesson, that I could do this without catching any feelings. I certainly didn't want a relationship just yet, but I wanted regular sex. I was like a pig in shit. Everything was perfect.

Unfortunately, my life never seems to be perfect for long. That weekend I bumped into his ex, Sarah, on a night out. Sarah is a beautiful, petite woman with eyes as fierce as a sphinx, accompanied by the most perfect winged eyeliner ever. We went to school together and like I said, we were not friends as such, but if we saw each other we would always say hello. The prosecco was flowing, and before we knew it we were deep into conversation. My body was riddled with guilt for sleeping with her ex, but as far as I knew, the relationship had finished a year ago. She then began to nervously say that she had something to tell me. It wasn't what I was expecting. She got her phone out and began to show me that Chris had been messaging her. "I haven't replied to him though, you have a child together. I wouldn't do that, " she said. I wanted the ground to swallow me whole. *Fuck. Do I tell her? Do I not? Am I lying to this woman's face if I don't? Fuck, fuck, fuck.*

Wait. It gets worse.

I decided to ask her about her love life, hoping she'd say she's madly in love with some man called Pierre from France because she's that type. But no. She tells me she is confused at the moment because she has been sleeping with her ex Aaron again – *oh my fucking God.*

Great, what the fuck have I got myself into? What the fuck do I do now? Do I break this woman's heart by telling her that

I'm also sleeping with him? I have been in some awkward positions, but this one was up there – maybe even in my top three. I felt terrible, embarrassed, ashamed and guilty. I felt everything all at once.

At that moment, I decided for both of our sakes to zip my mouth and lock away the key. My eyes started to wander nervously as the guilt was boiling up and then a sudden glimmer of sparkle stopped me in my tracks. *The diamond ring.* Of course it was *HER* fucking ring. She was obviously still crazy in love with this man, asking me if I had heard anything about him or knew anyone he had been with recently. I started to think that maybe she was trying to catch me out, but I don't think she had a clue. My mind was spiralling, so I decided to dig – I needed clarification. I asked her when was the last time she had slept with him.

"I went round Tuesday and Friday last week, " she said.

Holy shit. I was there on Monday and Thursday.

If I could have screamed it from the rooftops, I would have, but I couldn't. It was so messed up, I couldn't get my head around it. This man has some serious balls, I'll tell you… no pun intended! Do you know the first thing I thought? He wouldn't have even washed his bedsheets in between us. I felt like I was going to throw up. I had this sudden rage. Not because I liked him or saw us going somewhere, nothing like that, just at how disgusting he was. To not give a flying fuck. I wasn't even really thinking of myself. I was thinking of this oblivious woman in front of me. How could he do that to her?

At this point, she started really confiding in me, and I couldn't get out. I couldn't shut her down, so I just sat and listened to her. She told me that Aaron would text her expressing his love to her and that he'd changed and wanted to make it work. *WHAT?* He could have fucked me over no problem, slept with other women even, but to say that to his ex-girlfriend, trying to rekindle what they had while fucking me, was just so fucked up.

I know I should have told her, or I should have messaged him to tell her. After all, it was his mess, not mine. But I didn't. I didn't want or need the drama, so I decided to message Aaron begging him not to tell her or anyone that we had been sleeping together. I thought if we just kept it a secret, no one would get hurt. My message to him didn't stop there, though. I couldn't stop myself and wound up giving him some home truths about how much of a dog he had been. I told him that I really liked him as a person and didn't deserve to be lied to like that. Never mind his ex-girlfriend – she didn't deserve that. I wished him a very sarcastic good luck with it all, and do you want to know what he replied? He replied with a fucking emoji. The emoji of a man holding his hands up and shrugging, as if to say "oh well" or "oops". Not one single word. Not even an explanation or an apology. He didn't even want to defend himself. What an *arsehole.*

He loved asses so much, he became one.

~Unknown

A month went by, and I heard that Sarah and Aaron were back on. I was glad. I thought this meant Sarah had no idea about me, and I could go on living my life without her or anyone else ever knowing about us sleeping together. Until one evening, I was out having a drink with my friend and got the dreaded text: *Hey, it's Sarah, can you ring me when you get five minutes, please?*

Please, God, no. I was trying to live a life without drama, without any stress, but I owed it to her, I owed it to her to call her and listen to what she had to say, and let's be honest, I knew what she was ringing for.

Half an hour later, I returned her call. The tone of her voice was soft, not angry or aggressive, nothing but sweet and innocent. She began by saying she wouldn't ever have a problem with me, that I am single and can do whatever I want, and that she would never hate me, but ultimately she just needed to know the truth. *God, this woman really is a sweetheart.* I stayed utterly silent until she had gotten out everything she wanted to say. Then came the question. "Have you slept with Aaron recently?"

I took a deep breath and apologised from the bottom of my heart that I hadn't told her before. I'm surprised she understood a word I said. I was so nervous I spoke a hundred miles per hour. Even then, her tone didn't change towards me one bit. She was gutted though, she couldn't believe it. She began to tell me that someone had already told her, but she didn't want to bring me into it (*again, what a sweetheart*). But when she pulled Aaron up on it, he claimed he hadn't seen me in years, so she wanted to ask me. I want to say what a pig that he lied to her face, but on the other hand, I did beg him not to say anything, so I don't know if he was doing that for himself or me. We were on the phone for over an hour, talking about the situation and what she was going to do, and we even spoke about Chris. We both wished each other well and left with no animosity or bitterness.

It takes grace to remain kind in cruel situations.

~Rupi Kaur

So, my first experience of single life and this is what happens. I thought: This must just be a bit of bad luck, single life can't all be like this, can it? Not all men are going to be like this, are they? Surely most men have more respect for women than that? I knew I had made the right decision with leaving Chris, but my God, I did not want to be single if this was a taste of how a modern-day man acts. He could have easily said he was seeing someone or not even replied to my Instagram message, but no. I guess if it's on a plate for them, men like that are going to lick that plate clean… literally. I don't know what I was to Aaron, probably nothing more than a fuck buddy, probably just something to keep him entertained as he rekindled things with Sarah, or maybe I made him realise he did love her. I don't know, and I never will know, but I do know that it made me feel like complete and utter shit.

For years I'd been so used to being someone's only option, having a partner that didn't look at or even speak to another woman. Suddenly, I was single and had lost all control over how people act towards me. When you're single, you have no say, and you just have to accept it. You go from communicating and being completely honest to barefaced lies and deceit. It's one extreme to the other. It might sound easy to just get back out on the field, but it's not. It's adjusting to a completely different life, to entirely different people. You find yourself exposed to men that just disregard and disrespect you because they want to keep their options open. Guys don't realise what that does to a woman's self-esteem, to their confidence and their future views on men. The second I started to feel comfortable and self-confident, it got ripped from beneath me. Surely it couldn't get any worse than this…

When they talk about a knight in shining armour, they are not talking about the guy, ladies. You need to be the one wearing the armour. It's a fucking battlefield out there.

Chapter Six
The Regret

Drama does not just walk into our lives. Either we create it, invite it, or associate with it.

~Brandi L. Bates

Following the Aaron saga, I was still only looking to have some fun with no strings attached – nothing more. Ben seemed to be the perfect fit for precisely that, but he is one person I regret getting involved with because he caused so much drama. I didn't need hassle from something that was supposed to be casual and innocent. Buckle up – this gives *The Only Way Is Essex* a run for its money.

I had known Ben for a few years through mutual friends and would often see him on nights out. We'd once shared a taxi home and had a little kiss when I was single years earlier, but that was as far as it went. I was always attracted to him, though. He was just short of six feet tall, which is normally my cut off, but I wasn't on the lookout for a boyfriend, so it didn't matter. He had dirty blonde hair like mine and the most impeccable jawline. You know, if you had a list of people you wanted to have sex with, well, he would have been on mine.

Ever since becoming single I noticed Ben would reply to my Instagram stories, and when things finished with Aaron, I started to return replies. He quickly took the hint and sparked up a conversation asking how I was, and a few days later he asked to see me. He lived with his parents, so I invited him over to my house. The first man to step foot in my home since Chris left – a detail I quickly pushed to the back of my mind. Ben was so confident, he charged through the front door without knocking or even announcing his arrival. Instead, he came in, bouncing off the walls and screeching through a mouthful of blinding white veneers, "You alright, babe?" He didn't even take his shoes off at the front door, which is an absolute bugbear of mine!

I always knew his personality could be overpowering – he made me look quiet, and that's saying something! To his credit he was also amusing, the life and soul of any party and always had a story to tell. The more time I spent with Ben, the more he seemed to calm down. He became a lot softer, less guarded and easier to talk to. I remember feeling like I was seeing a different side to him. *Boy, oh boy, I had no idea just how many more sides of his personality would emerge.*

Earlier in the year, there had been a rumour floating around that Ben was having an affair with a married Australian model called Megan, whose husband was also a model, both living in London. Megan was a friend of my friends. We knew each other by association but were absolutely not friends ourselves. I had met her a few times in big groups at people's birthdays or social events, but that was it. I always got a negative vibe when I was around her, the type that would drain every inch of you. She comes across as the kind of woman who won't stop until she gets what she wants, and she doesn't let anyone get in her way. She is strikingly attractive with a body that looks like it was carved by angels and she has this powerful aura about her. Whenever she walks into a room, people seem to be drawn to her. Or maybe it's just the way she looks.

Not me though, she's never been my cup of tea. I remember once she approached me at a social event. She didn't even say hello before telling me that I needed my breasts doing again. She later claimed she said it in a friendly way – although I'm not sure how exactly. You see, the city I live in is so small that everyone knows everyone, and it sometimes feels like everyone has slept with everyone too. You can't meet anyone without knowing somebody that has already been with them. So when

Ben came over, I asked him outright if the rumour was true. I didn't want to get myself into another sticky situation and certainly not with Megan, who had already left a bad taste in my mouth. He swore it wasn't true; that the rumour came from them being flirty on a night out the previous year, but it was hands down just hearsay. He seemed legit, so I took what he said as the truth.

Ben was quite touchy-feely from the get-go, and the more wine we had, the more intimate the night got. We never would have been able to watch a film or anything on the telly, Christ – I imagine he is one of those annoying people that interrupt every two minutes asking what is going on – but we talked and laughed for hours. I can generally read men quite well and tell whether they're going to be good in bed or not, but Ben, I couldn't read him at all. I don't know what it was, maybe I thought he was too confident, that he must be overcompensating because down there isn't that great, but I kept thinking: *Fuck, is this going to be the worst shag of my life?* Oh how he surprised me…

Please don't be gentle with me, she whispered, I want you to push my knees apart and paint my thighs With purple kisses.

~Michael Faudet

His personality reflected his approach to sex. He was like an excitable, rampant rabbit. But I didn't complain. The more he wanted it, the more I wanted it. We had sex five or six times that night. He knew exactly how I wanted it – rough and hard. The bruises he left were even bigger and darker than Aaron left me with. Bright red handprints from bursting small superficial blood vessels over my arse, dark purple love bites around my inner thighs, my neck and my breasts. At this point, I didn't even have a bed. I had sold the majority of the things in the house when Chris left; it didn't seem right to have someone else in that bed after he had been in it for years. But my new bed wasn't due to arrive for another six weeks, so the mattress took a pounding instead. I mean, it was probably a good thing because I'm pretty sure my bed wouldn't have survived the night.

We slept for no more than four hours before Ben's alarm went off for work. He was all over me like a rash, saying he didn't want to leave and go to work. So he rang in, made an excuse and said he would be a few hours late, so he could lie in bed with me for a little while longer. Well, that's not entirely accurate – it was so he could stay inside me a bit longer.

It was high school shit, really – carefree, fun and exciting, and it kept me from feeling lonely. A few days later, Ben called to ask why I had been slow at replying. "I like someone who keeps me on my toes, someone who is a bit hard to get, " I said bravely. He put the phone down. I guess he was trying to regain some control and be what I wanted him to be. I remember calling Amy and explaining that I felt like I would get the "ick" soon because of all the messages. She told me to play it cool with Ben to avoid getting the ick, so I made excuses and kept saying I was busy when he asked to see me.

The following Friday night I was at the pub with my friend Lucy. We went back to hers to carry on drinking, and while I was there Ben messaged to say he was desperate to see me. He had been on his Christmas night out with work and was more than forty-five minutes away, but it didn't stop him from getting a taxi straight to Lucy's house to see me.

I stumbled down her cobbled road and met him at the bottom of the street to jump into the black cab to take us both back to mine. Even though I wasn't sure how I felt about Ben, when I was around him, I was instantly wet. I couldn't control how horny he made me feel and how much I just kept wanting sex. Within seconds of being in the taxi I'd straddled him, grinding my hips back and forth as we passionately kissed. The next thing I knew, he flung me around, unzipping my high-waisted trousers, pulling them down to my thighs. His hands gripped either side of my hips, and he gently placed me onto his hard penis. The rhythm got quicker and quicker; whipping my hair across his face from behind, I rode him vigorously, truly living up to the dirty bitches that have sex in the back of a taxi. God knows what the driver must have thought. He definitely got more than he bargained for that night. But I was blind drunk, and quite frankly, I didn't give a fuck. We arrived back at mine before long, rushing straight upstairs as if he hadn't just been inside me, and had another night of endless sex until five o'clock in the morning.

After just a few hours of sleep, I woke up dehydrated and hungover. After having sex probably seven times, I told him how sore I was and that I couldn't take anymore. But with his hands on my body, the second those fingers went down on me, I was wet again. I don't know what it was he did to me. This time, we had the slowest, most sensual sex. And it lasted ages. The rhythm didn't quicken – it never got rough. It was just deep, passionate sex: looking into each other's eyes, moaning softly into each other's mouths as I gripped the back of his hair tighter and tighter with each thrust.

Halfway through, I could feel word vomit coming up. "Is this weird?" I blurted out.

He laughed, replying: "A bit, but it's fucking great." It had been such a long time since I had had sex like that. It was as if it was meaningful. As if we liked each other. Or that he liked me.

Sometimes she likes gentle and intimate other times she needs rough and animalistic and being able to decipher which she needs and when is part of the art of being a man?

~J. M. Storm

A couple of weeks later, Ben and I wound up going to a Christmas market with a group of mutual friends, where everything began to unfold. I had severe anxiety that morning because I didn't know how to act around him in public, but I needn't have worried. Straight away, we were all over each other. Even our friends commented, "You two look perfect together" and "Get a room!" Even though they made me feel at ease and comfortable, I didn't care that the rest of the world could see us too, and he didn't seem to either. It was like we were blind to the world.

Every chance we got, we were snogging each other's faces. Every time we went outside for a cigarette he would pin me against the wall, kiss my neck, hoist one of my legs up and press himself against me so I could feel how hard he was. I was getting drunker and drunker and, of course, hornier by the second, so like the carefree, irresponsible people we had become, we decided to have sex in the toilets of the bar we were in. It might sound like I had lost my dignity by that point, but I didn't see it like that. I saw it as two people who just couldn't keep their hands off each other. Two very drunk people, I should add.

The night was getting on and we moved to the next bar. We went out for another cigarette, and that's when my panicked, serious side started to emerge. "I don't know what this is Ben, I don't do this. It always turns messy just sleeping with someone. I've just come out of a relationship. I don't know if this is too much."

He grabbed my face. "Listen, I don't care if you wake up tomorrow and think differently and want to stop this, then that's OK, I will respect that, but if you don't, then let's just carry on doing what we are doing. I really like you Elle, and I don't want what we have going on to finish."

Slightly worried I had gotten into this way too fast and in too deep, I decided to knock the conversation on the head and go back inside. The drinks were still flowing and I sat back into the corner of the booth, which meant I couldn't easily get out. Being playful, I gently nudged Ben's leg with my foot. "Can you get me a drink, please, babe?" I asked.

To my horror, he grabbed my ankle with force, looked me sternly in the face and barked: "Don't you ever fucking kick me again… ever!"

Half of me thought he was joking, so I asked multiple times, "Are you joking right now?" I tried to quickly explain that I didn't mean to kick him, that it was just the silly person he knew I was. I was still confused about how much he had overreacted when he furiously demanded that I apologise: "Say sorry NOW!"

Standing my ground, I told him no, he needed to apologise to *me*. His voice was getting louder and angrier because I wouldn't back down. I know I am a deeply apologetic person, but when someone has tried to call me out on something so innocent and playful, my severely stubborn side comes out. We really were like a pair of teenagers. Arguing for what seemed like an eternity, we both apologised, and I muttered under my breath, "That's why we would never be together. We just clash."

He heard me and walked off to get the drink I didn't even want anymore. I knew in that second that he was too immature for me. We were both obviously powerful characters and had big personalities that meant we clashed, but he scared me too.

Women want a man who is in control, but not a man who is controlling. There's a difference.

~J. M. Storm

Trying to forget everything that just happened, we played some drinking games to lighten the mood and things felt somewhat back to normal. That's the thing with alcohol; you can feel so strongly about something one minute, and then the next, you've forgotten all about it. It was coming up to two o'clock in the morning and we had been drinking since noon, so we decided to order a taxi to go home. I quickly went to the toilet as everyone made their way outside, and when I returned, Ben's body language had changed entirely. I asked him what was wrong. "It's her. She's texted me, " he nervously replied.

Who? I thought. And then it clicked, it was written all over his face: *Megan.*

The two of us got straight into the back of the taxi and not holding back for a second longer, I asked, "So the rumours were true then?" He confessed to me and started to explain that it had been over for a long time, but that little brain of mine was already ticking. If it had been over for a long time, why was she still messaging him? *Here we go again,* I thought, *déjà fucking vu.*

He could tell my mood had shifted and that I was pissed off. I mean, who wouldn't be? You've just fucked a guy in the toilets, and now his "mistress" or whatever is texting him. But the difference was, he was showing me all her messages. He was really trying to prove that he wasn't bothered anymore. She saw that we were out together on social media and messaged him, saying he was disrespectful for having a good time with *her* friends. He wasn't disrespectful. She was just jealous. He pleaded with me to not let her texts have an effect on us. "Please don't let her bother you. I really want to wake up to you in the morning, " he said.

He tried to make me feel better. Whether this was his form of an apology or he really did just have one thing on his mind, he got his way. There his hands were again, in the taxi, making me soaking wet. We were more discreet this time. Well, I say that, but I'm pretty sure everyone knew we were having sex. They were all just drunk or turned a blind eye to it by singing and dancing.

He stayed at mine, and I acted like everything was normal even though it wasn't. The lines were so blurred. I'd seen a different side to him that night, and now there was this daunting feeling that his ex was back in the picture or had maybe never left. I could sense that there was drama on the horizon, and I knew he did too. The next morning, I drove him home, and we didn't speak a word to each other for two days.

It was Christmas Eve, and I still hadn't heard from him. Don't get me wrong, I hadn't tried to speak to him either. Amy and Lucy were going to the pub so I decided to join them for a couple of drinks. I hadn't been there ten minutes when one of the girls turned to me and said, "She knows." They were, of course, referring to Megan. Turns out he couldn't lie to her as well as he had lied to me and he had confessed to sleeping with me.

Multiple people told me not to worry; that I had done nothing wrong. I wasn't worried. Megan and I weren't friends, Ben and I were both single, and she supposedly still had a husband. But something didn't sit right. I could tell by their look of panic that this was the start of something bigger, that this wasn't going to go down well with Megan. It was as if the mood had changed entirely and there was a black cloud hanging over me, threatening a downpour. I felt immediately uncomfortable, like all of a sudden I was an outsider and these women that I had been spending so much time with instantly didn't want to know me. Then the rush of guilt entered me. Even though they hadn't given any inclination that what Ben and I were doing was an issue, and they even supported it in some respects, I had a wave of guilt come over me as if I really shouldn't have gone there.

Ben was joining everyone at the pub that evening. A huge part of me just wanted to leave; I didn't have anything to say to him and I didn't want to be involved in whatever was about to kick off. I tried to leave, but before I could he walked in. He came straight over to me and asked if I was alright. "Well, you wouldn't know if I was alright because you haven't spoken to me in two days. Anyway, I know she knows about us – did you not fancy giving me the heads up?"

Drunk and slurring his words, he said he wanted to tell me face to face and that he was sorry for dragging me into the situation. Only he wasn't apologising. He was just warming me up for what came next. "If Megan asks you, can you please tell her that we only slept together once, that we were really drunk after a night out?"

Are you fucking kidding me right now? I was irritated and repulsed by this, and I just wanted out. I couldn't believe I had gotten myself into another situation like this. Another love triangle, without the fucking love part!

Amy was enraged. I told her not to waste her energy, but she's my best friend and she knew deep down that regardless of whether I liked him or not, his comments would have hurt me. So she went in – screaming and shouting at him, furious at how he dared to ask me to lie for the sake of a married woman. That he'd been brainwashed by her and that he should never have got involved with me if he knew she would have a problem with it.

Everything was getting extremely loud. I couldn't face what was unravelling in front of me, so I left to meet my other friends, hoping that I would never speak to Ben again, or have to talk about the situation. Aside from Amy, all these other so-called friends sat there and buried their heads in the sand, so I left without saying goodbye.

The next day, Ben texted me: *Merry Christmas, Elle. I apologise for all the shit that's kicked off. I should have given you a heads up.*

I kept my reply short: *What's done is done. It's fine. Merry Christmas.*

I had no energy to entertain the situation – no great essay, nothing. I just wanted to draw a line under it. Deep down, I knew I couldn't have liked him that much if I didn't feel the need to send one of my infamous wordy paragraphs. I knew that it was too much too soon and that I was already starting to get the ick, but I guess I had gotten wrapped up in the moment. And with it being Christmas, that didn't help. I didn't want to be alone.

On Boxing Day, I was with my family at my brother's house when there was a call from an unknown number. It was Megan. She said she wanted to make sure that I knew that she didn't have a problem with me, as she didn't want to feel awkward in any situation further down the line if we were all in the same room together. "If you want to sleep with him again and carry things on, then that's fine by me, " she claimed. She told me she really didn't care about Ben and that she was trying to make it work with her husband, so if Ben and I wanted to, we could carry on. There was just one catch – if we *did* carry on, she wanted to know. Being careful not to divulge too many details, I told her it had just been a bit of fun, that it had happened more than once, but there was nothing more to it, and we wouldn't be sleeping together again.

Then in came three missed calls from Ben. I didn't want to call him back, so I messaged him: *I'm guessing you're only ringing me because you've heard from Megan?* He said he wanted to know what I had told her. *Ask her*, I replied bluntly. *I don't want to be involved.*

Unfortunately, it was too late, and before I knew it, the whole thing became a fucking circus. I was receiving calls and messages from all of our mutual friends. Everyone was trying to act like they didn't know, asking me to lie and say that no one else knew. It was bullshit. Everyone was running for cover from Megan because no one wanted to be on the wrong side of her, and they would obviously drop everyone else to please her. But I refused to bow down to her. I hadn't done anything wrong but I was still being thrown under the bus. Remember, I hadn't known they'd had an affair, but it became clearer that other people had.

Entertain a clown, and you become part of the circus.

~Unknown

Then the begging started. "Can we please agree that you lied and that the sex only happened once, but we shared a few kisses after?" He told me he didn't want the hassle. *He* didn't want the hassle. What about me? I was trying to enjoy Boxing Day with my family, and this mess was ruining it. He even told me he would bring me a souvenir back from his holiday if I lied for him. *What am I, ten years old?* It was embarrassing, and he kept asking the same question over and over again.

I tried to squash the conversation and stopped replying, but two hours later, I received more messages: *Shit is hitting the fan, Elle. Look, if she asks, we haven't spoken today, OK?* More lies. What the fuck was this woman doing to him? All hell had broken loose – not only between Megan and Ben but between Megan and her girlfriends too. She was livid because they knew he had slept with me but hadn't told her. She made them feel terrible about it, playing the victim, and it drew them even further apart from me. Let me reiterate, she still had a husband at this point.

Ben was backtracking more than ever. He didn't want any evidence that we had even spoken, after all the things he said.

I quickly went from not giving a fuck to feeling like a total mug, and lost my shit. I couldn't let it go without defending myself.

Shaking with anger, I text him: *I am not just some whore that you fucked and get to say you fucked after a drunken night out where you didn't know what you were doing. No. I have done nothing wrong. I am not lying to anybody.* He had become so desperate it was cringeworthy, but I'm sorry, I was standing my ground. I wasn't just going to be a pawn in some fucked up affair. I was not being treated and seen that way.

I asked him why he had said those things to me at the Christmas market if I was such a dirty little secret?

He replied: *I don't ever remember saying that to you. I must have been pissed.*

Wow. This man was a fucking *dickhead.* I fiercely told him to never speak to me again, and warned him that if he did, I wouldn't reply.

Later that day, I noticed he'd blocked me on Instagram. I'm not complaining, I was relieved if anything, but shouldn't it have been the other way round? Megan had well and truly mind-fucked him. Maybe that felt like a victory to her, I don't know. Perhaps she felt like she had won because he had chosen her. But I felt like the real winner. I thought, *you can keep Ben the Bullshitter.* I stayed true to myself and stood my ground, even at the risk of losing friends. Christ, I was never looking to run into the sunset hand in hand with this guy.

Honesty is a very expensive gift. Don't expect it from cheap people.

~Warren Buffett

Two days after Boxing Day, I was going out with the same bunch of friends that knew Megan. That morning, I was told by one of my friends (with whom I have been close with for sixteen years) not to come because Megan was going. *How come I am the one who is being shut out? You were all egging me on in the Ben situation, and now you want to turn your back on me?*

Still, I decided not to go. Amy was infuriated at the situation, but I told her to still go, so she did. Shocked but also not surprised, I got a phone call from her at ten o'clock asking me to pick her up because she'd got into a blazing argument with Megan. Again, she was the only one to stick up for me, whilst all the others sat on the fence. Well, they didn't even sit on the fence – in their eyes, there was no fence. It was Megan's side or no side. I never wanted people to choose me. It was never about choosing; it was about how my so-called friends could be all for me one minute and drop me like a sack of shit the next because they were too terrified to stand their ground.

These were the only friends that knew all this was going on. They were the only ones that I felt like I could talk to and see. When Amy travelled back home to Newcastle, I felt like I had no one. This is why this one was different. I could get past the fact that Ben dropped me for a model that had a husband – more fool him – but it hurt that my friends dropped me, and that's a different kind of hurt. I had just been through this whirlwind of an experience, and Megan was smug as sin with Ben on one arm and my friends on the other. Fuck knows where her husband was going to fit.

Maybe Ben and Megan were in love, I don't know. Whatever they had, there were clearly more feelings involved than there ever was between us. Even though I didn't want to be with him, I still struggle to understand how someone could say those things and so quickly take them back. Words are cheap, and I guess so are the mouths of some of the people that they come from. I never agreed to take part in a competition, but that is what it wound up as. I was beginning to think that single life wasn't for me. When they talk about your knight in shining armour, they are not talking about the guy, ladies. You need to be the one wearing the armour. It's a fucking battlefield out there.

I don't know what I was thinking. In fact, I wasn't thinking at all. I felt like my body had been swapped with one I didn't even recognise.

Chapter Seven
The Friend Zone

Always pity the thinkers, for they are cursed with their own imagination.

~Atticus

Liam and I have been friends for years. He is, without a doubt, one of the nicest people I have ever known and had the privilege of having in my life. He is hilarious, caring, thoughtful… the list goes on – all the things you actually want in a boyfriend. I would even go as far as to say that he's husband material.

When I jetted off to America, Liam happened to be passing through San Francisco on his travels on the week leading up to Valentine's Day. There we were, two friends, both on the other side of the world and both single, so we thought, fuck it, let's go out together for a little "date night". The evening escalated quickly, turning from drinks to jumping into the pool at one of the world's most beautiful and famous bars. Then, like the classy people we were, we obviously wound up in McDonald's in the early hours– where else would you want to spend Valentine's night? We went our separate ways after our Big Macs, and that was that. When Chris and I got back together, Liam and I remained friends, and I would often see him over drinks or at friends' birthdays and social events. It was an ongoing joke about our little Valentine's date, with him telling people that I "friend-zoned" him.

We met up a couple of times after my final split with Chris – always just for a casual drink down the pub with mutual friends. But on one occasion, it was a particularly heavy night. We bought more alcohol from the local shop to carry on the night, and things soon escalated with one of my friends throwing up in the sink. We all ended up staying the night – the other two were a couple, so they stayed in Liam's spare room, and I stayed in his bed with him. Without an inch of romance or flirting, we talked about my newly single life, and he told me about his. We turned over, and within seconds, we were both snoring.

Then, New Year's Eve arrived.

In hindsight, I could see a breakdown coming a mile off. Drink had become my best friend. I wasn't an alcoholic by any means; it could be one glass at night, or it could be a bottle. Whatever it was, it numbed the pain. Not only was all the drama unfolding with Ben, but there was a lot more that was happening behind the scenes. My brother proposed to his girlfriend on Christmas Day morning, as we were driving up to Liverpool to spend it with them. When we got there she showed me her ring, and I couldn't stop myself from bursting into tears. It came from the pit of my stomach and a deep, dark place of sadness mixed with envy, but I had to pretend they were happy tears. After we were all in the house, Noah playing with his new toys and me slumped on the sofa with a stinking hangover, they played a video of my brother proposing. I could feel the tears rolling down my face. Again, I was doing my best to pretend they were happy tears when really, they were not. I adore his girlfriend, and she was already like a sister to me. I so wanted to be happy for them, but I found it impossible.

Social media was also destroying me. I didn't want to see these people on their amazing family holidays or see all the gifts they received on Christmas Day when it felt like all I had was more alcohol to indulge in. And God forbid I saw one more person post about being pregnant! Having to look at everyone playing happy families over Christmas and New Year was heart-breaking. I wanted to think it wasn't jealously because I knew I didn't want that – after all, that's the reason why I was in this mess – but it was. It was the bright green-eyed monster, jealously. I started to resent the people I loved, just because they were in a good place in their lives and I wasn't.

I feel heavy because my heart absorbs everything around me.

~Bridgett Devoue

Soon enough, it was New Year's Eve: the night you're supposed to leave the past behind you and look forward to the future. I made a last-minute decision to go to the local pub where I met my parents for a drink before my friends arrived. By six o'clock, I had already cried to my parents, and I realise now I should have taken myself home at that point. But no, I stayed, fully intending to get "white girl wasted". I wanted to forget all the drama of the last few months, every bit of heartache and hurt – I wanted to leave it all behind in that year. That didn't exactly go to plan, but I did manage to get wasted and forget everything that evening. I didn't even stay with my friends the entire night. I was clinging on to people I had known from school and word vomiting everything that had happened to me after the climb to anyone who would listen. I can't tell you how many times I cried, but it was a lot.

As midnight approached I decided I needed a New Year's kiss, so what did I do? I decided to kiss a guy who just so happened to be one of Chris' old friends in front of everyone. Bitch, I know. Being drunk is no excuse. I don't know what I was thinking. In fact, I wasn't thinking at all. I felt like my body had been swapped with one I didn't even recognise.

Then I got invited to an afterparty at Liam's house. Things proceeded to go from bad to worse. There was a point in the night that I blacked out for two hours, and even now, I cannot remember a single thing. That shit is scary, and a position I never, ever want to be in again. It was around four o'clock when Liam chucked everyone out. I didn't know what I was doing at this point, but I came downstairs to see that everyone had gone. Because I had slept there before and nothing happened, I felt comfortable staying over again that night.

We went outside for a cigarette and I briefly remember sobbing, pouring my heart out to him. I can't remember exactly what was said. You would probably have to ask him, but I know I was a mess. The walk from outside to his back door to the bedroom was a bit of a blur. We crawled into bed, and before I knew it he had leaned in for a kiss. Being emotional and craving attention, I didn't say no. Not only was this a low point because I had just been crying my eyes out (I dread to think what I looked like), but I wasn't prepared for sex. I purposely hadn't shaved to stop myself from being tempted, but that soon went out the window. I even had two bras on… *TWO BRAS!* I was wearing a white blazer dress which showed my cleavage, so I had a nude-coloured one that pushed my breasts up and a black lace one over the top so you could see it under my dress. I also had Spanx on, for fuck's sake. Well, they soon came off and even better, I never recovered them, so that must have been a nice little souvenir for him to remember me by. *How embarrassing.* Not that he would have noticed any of these things or even cared; he was as drunk as me. I know I like to think I'm a bit of a porn star when I've had a drink, so the only good thing that came out of it was that I probably gave him the shag of his year and started the new year off with a bang… literally.

Thankfully it wasn't awkward the next morning. I was so glad – I would have hated for our friendship to have been ruined by a drunken hook-up. I lied to my dad and got him to pick me up down the road, so off I trotted in my high-heeled boots, my white dress that was no longer white thanks to the stains all down it and black panda eyes from all the crying. Talk about having flashbacks – I felt like I'd gone right back to my days of doing the walk of shame at university. Only I wasn't at university now, and I couldn't help but think I should have known better. I went home to slump in my own self-pity and anxiety.

Drinking alcohol is like pouring gasoline on your anxiety.

~Laura McKowen

After Liam, I felt the worst I had ever felt in all the months I had been single. I felt so alone. Nothing could fill my happiness, not even sex. I hadn't cried a lot after the breakup until this point. I mean, I *had* cried, don't get me wrong, but this was different. This one was a heart-wrenching, soul-destroying, on-the-bathroom-floor cry. I thought to myself, *how am I ever going to be okay? How am I ever going to pick myself up from the emptiness I feel inside?* I had the most amazing little boy in front of my eyes, but even he couldn't fill the void; nothing could make me feel better.

I needed to get my head together for both my sake and for Noah's, or I felt like my life could seriously spiral out of control, and I could end up being an unfit mother. It's different when you only have yourself to look after, but when you're responsible for another human being, you have no choice but to pick yourself back up. Before I did this, I had one more fuck up to make…

You can't just turn your feelings off for someone. I wish there was a switch, but there isn't.

Chapter Eight
The Heartbreaker

Whatever you do, never run back to what broke you.

~Frank Ocean

Max was the man who tore my heart to pieces. It was the beginning of summer and I had moved back to my parents after finishing university. It had only been a month since I'd split up from Chris. I was the thinnest I have ever been with bleach blonde locks nearly touching my bum, full of tacky hair extensions. I was out with a couple of my best friends, and the second I saw Max, I was hooked. He was tall with long, dirty blonde hair, bright blue eyes and a rough look about him that I couldn't resist.

Last orders were called at the bar, so I went over to get our final round in. I could instantly feel his eyes on me. We went back and forth with eye contact as I kept looking to my left and looking away nervously until I dove in with "Do I know you?" The conversation was flowing, and before we knew it the club was closing and we were the only ones left at the bar. The girls were walking to the exit shouting for me to hurry up as they wanted to go to McDonald's, so he asked for my number, and I hurried away.

The second we got into the queue, a message from an unknown number came through. It was Max. We shared a few flirty messages. Then he said: *I'm doing forty days and forty nights of no sex, or I'd ask you to come over.*

I'd had a belly full of courage (as well as alcohol and chicken nuggets), so I wrote straight back: *Bet I can break that.* The idea must have excited him because he instantly sent me his address and told me to get in a taxi.

When I arrived at his flat we went straight to his bedroom, and he explained that he was on day thirty-five and he wasn't going to break – but I could still stay over if I wanted. It took me ten minutes. Ten minutes to break him. He ripped the white lace knickers I was wearing in half, and that was the start of the most fucked up situation I have ever been in.

Romance is all well and good, but… it's just that I am not in the mood for whispered sweet nothings or your fingers running softly through my hair. What I want, more than anything, is for you to treat me like your own personal sex doll. Don't kiss me – make me bite my lip.

~Michael Faudet

After that first night, there was no question about us wanting to see each other again. Max was always honest – maybe a bit too honest. From day dot, he said he didn't want a girlfriend, and I agreed I did not want a boyfriend, but we both wanted regular sex. Friends with benefits seemed so easy in the beginning. But that's what we agreed it would be, with the simple caveat that if either of us started to develop feelings, we would tap out. But that's the thing about friends with benefits. Sooner or later, one of you will want to tap the fuck out.

Max and I got on famously. We were remarkably similar in a lot of ways. We were both really into music, we dressed alike and we were both impulsive and adventurous. Our mutual friends always said we were very well suited. Before things went south, we became incredibly good friends. I saw him most weeks, whether it was stone-cold sober or following a night out. I could talk to him about anything, and I did, for hours on end some nights, putting the world to rights. He would confide in me about his family, and I would do the same. I was still living with my parents at this point, so whenever I needed or wanted to get away, I would go to his. We were both really honest about our pasts and about our exes. He told me that he'd had his heart ripped to pieces years ago and that he never wanted to give someone else the chance to do that again. He was incredibly open, and unlike most men he was outright in telling me he wasn't ready for a relationship. One thing he did keep from me, however, was how much I reminded him of his ex-girlfriend – he didn't tell me that until later down the line. Maybe that's why it went the way it did.

The sex… the sex was so good; it was addictive. There wasn't much that we didn't try. Think *50 Shades of Grey* – except ours was fast becoming *50 Shades of Fucked Up*. I didn't realise at the time that even sex was a huge game to him. Take, for example, the fact that we never kissed. I know what you're thinking. How on earth do you have sex without kissing? But this was our form of knowing where we stood with each other because kissing makes sex intimate, so we agreed we would never kiss.

I never understood desire until I felt your hands around my throat.

~Michael Faudet

I bet you're wondering how things ever got started?

Well, just like Mr Grey, Max was a dominant. He would tell me what to do, and I would obey. I was, as they call it, his submissive. I was never allowed to wear clothes in his bed, so each time I went over, I would undress first without any interaction and lie on his bed in my underwear. He would tell me to start fingering myself, so I would. His body lying next to me, I would grab his hand while he watched me, indicating for him to take over and start pleasuring me. But he wouldn't move. Staying fixated on me, he wouldn't flinch until I begged him.

Within weeks, he asked me to bring my box of toys with me. I have always admired my toy box. I must have been one of Ann Summers' best customers. I had a vast range of different types of dildos, handcuffs, lube, anal beads, bullets – you name it, I had it. He would make me fuck myself with one of my vibrators in front of him, and every time I was about to climax, he would take it out of me so I wouldn't have an orgasm. He would do this multiple times so that when he finally let me, it was like an explosion. He would tease me until my dying breath. There would be times where he wouldn't leave a hole unaccounted for. I used to think he was the most selfless person in the world, always wanting to please me, but it was all just a fucked-up game of control.

On one occasion, I pulled up to his drive and texted him to say I was outside but had forgotten the box. As punishment, he ordered me to send a video of me pleasuring myself in the car, or I wasn't allowed in. If we were sober, the rule when I walked through the front door was to immediately go into his bedroom. If we stumbled through his front door after a night out, we would rarely make it to his bedroom. We got water from the kitchen, but on the way, he would bend me over his sofa, pull my dress up and fuck me. And that would just be the starter until we got into bed.

As I said, we liked our music, so we would lie in bed and listen to all kinds of music for hours on end, but the second he put Drake on, I knew it was about to go down. It was our love-making music, just without the love part. If the song was upbeat, the sex was fast and hard. If it was a slow jam, we would grind to the rhythm.

After months of building trust, he knew I would do anything he wanted, so he introduced his belt. *Oh, the belt.* He would set up his Apple MacBook to record, before bending me over, as I awaited him to reach for the black leather belt that he kept under his bed. The choice of where this belt was going to go was never mine, but he either had it tightly wrapped around my neck or he would use it to whip my bare arse. The pain was unlike any other sexual experience I had felt before. The burning sensation of being whipped in the same place over and over again, piercing my skin, leaving me red-raw and sore, was so pleasurable. He made sure we had a safe word, but I never used it. My entire body would be sensitive to his touch, and within seconds of him entering me, I would scream out and orgasm.

We were in such a routine. As soon as we were finished, I would throw on one of his baggy t-shirts and we would make our way to his kitchen and have a cigarette. I would lean over his countertop as the nicotine hit my lungs, my legs shaking like a leaf, struggling to put my full weight on them. I didn't know which was more addictive.

The sex was so good even the neighbours had a cigarette.

~Unknown

We became so comfortable around each other. We would shower together intending to wash, but it always ended up with me pressed against the shower tiles with his hands around my neck. There were Sundays where he left me asleep while he went to play rugby and would wake me up by going down on me. I just couldn't get enough of him. When we weren't having sex, listening to music or talking, we would lie there for hours, binge-watching episodes of our favourite programmes. Once I even forced him to watch all seven of the *Saw* movies, all in one day. He knew horror films were my thing, so after watching one at two o'clock in the morning, he threw on his red high top Converse, and I pulled on my pink high-tops, and we went to the graveyard near his apartment to scare the shit out of each other. It was playful and exciting, and we really were nailing the friends with benefits thing.

The strange thing was, he would tweet about me or to me and publicly comment on my Instagram pictures. It wasn't as if he wanted to hide the fact we were friends or sleeping with each other. He even wrote on a picture of me wearing knee-high socks, "Can't wait to wrap them around your neck." *Brave, hey?* But we were never allowed to go for food because that was too serious, and he didn't want people to think we were together.

On one occasion, there was a group of us at his place. We couldn't decide on a takeaway, so we went for a McDonalds. He had sheer anxiety at the thought of being seen out in public eating with me, but the second we got back to his, we took one sofa, and our friends took the other ready to watch a film, and we cuddled for the first time. Lying horizontally across the sofa, his body was behind mine with his arm over me through the entire film.

I started to realise he was giving me mixed signals, and I was confused about what he wanted from me. He didn't want anyone to think we were a couple or be seen out in public together, but it was OK to plaster himself all over my social media and be seen leaving bars and nightclubs together. He wouldn't kiss me, but he would cuddle me as if we were an item. My mind was in constant overdrive. *Was he starting to fall for me like I was for him?* I think that's the problem with fuck-buddy scenarios – usually, one of you will start to fall for the other. It's human nature when you spend all that time with someone. Not only are you connecting physically, but you are also getting to know them on an emotional level too. In this scenario it was me who was falling, and hard.

We'd been seeing each other for about five months when I decided it was time to tap out, so I did what I do best. I sent him an essay-long text message saying it was time to call it a day because I was scared my feelings were getting in the way, and I didn't want to get hurt.

But I was lying to myself. I was already in way too deep. I remember his reply like it was yesterday. He asked me why I would ruin something good and why did I have to catch feelings? He was blaming me.

Deep down, all I wanted was for him to turn around and say he'd caught feelings too and for us to give this a shot. But he didn't. He couldn't. And that wasn't the end of it. He didn't respect my feelings whatsoever. He continued to ask me over, knowing I wouldn't say no. He would tell me to "man up" and switch off my feelings – like it was that easy. After that, I stupidly told him I never meant what I said, but he knew exactly how I felt, and he used it against me.

I just wanted you to fuck me,
And then I became greedy,
I wanted you to love me.

~Tracey Emin

I was in total limbo, falling for a guy who couldn't give me what I wanted but feeling like I couldn't end it. It was all the worse because he didn't want it to end either. To try to regain some control, I slept with someone else. I wanted to see Max's reaction to see if he would get mad. But he didn't get mad. He got furious. And then the head-fucking really started to roll. "If you hadn't slept with that guy, then I would have given us a real shot, but you've fucked it now."

Rather than face the problem head-on, we decided to start having sex with other people while continuing our fucked-up situation. He'd ask me over later and later. It would be one or two o'clock sometimes (a booty call if I've ever seen one before), but I would be there at his beck and call. We both wanted to carry things on, but it was so toxic.

Almost every Saturday night, we would go back home with each other. If we didn't, we knew the other one was sleeping with someone else. He once sent me a text to see where I was. I told him I was in a taxi on the way to a hotel with an actor I'd met at a party. He was livid and sent me several pictures of him in bed with another woman. So, I did the same back. It was completely and utterly poisonous, but I kept going back to him. Each time he told me to jump, I would ask how high – I knew exactly what he was doing to me but I couldn't let go. He was the kind of guy you want to save. You know, you want to be that girl that finally makes him settle down after all those years, to change his ways. I used to say he was a bad egg. He was even saved in my phone with the red cross emoji and an egg. He wasn't actually a bad person, but he was for me. We were really bad for each other.

One night, I was walking out of a club with Max when we saw Aaron (remember we'd had a one-night stand all those years ago?) in the smoking area. Following Max like a little puppy, we went over and the men shook hands. "Is this awkward for you?" Max asked. I could feel my face turning the shade of a tomato.

"No, not at all, " I lied.

Then he turned to Aaron and said, "She's a good shag, though, isn't she?"

What did he just say?

"Yes, mate, very decent, " was Aaron's response.

I felt so degraded as they both sniggered at my expense. I was mortified. Completely humiliated. Did I go back to Max's apartment that night? Of course I did. He had this crazy hold over me. It was so messy; there were nights where his sister started on me, where my brother started on him. We had told each of them our sides of the story, so my brother hated him and his sister hated me. But even after those fights, we still went home together. It ended so many times for us. I would beg him to leave me alone, but then he would text me days later, saying: *You done being a sap yet?* And like clockwork, I would go back. He was fucking up my whole life. I was miserable.

Everything I did was to get a reaction from him or for his approval. I started to go to raves because I knew he would be there and think I was "cool", even though they really were not my cup of tea. I had a very well-paid steady job at the time, and I got sacked because one day I didn't turn up. I stayed at his place but didn't get to sleep until the early hours of the morning and I forgot to set my alarm. We woke up at noon. At that moment, being in bed with him meant more to me than a job. Every inch of me was obsessed with him.

After months of torment, I couldn't take it anymore and wanted to run away. I couldn't deal with knowing about all these other women he was sleeping with. I was stalking their social media, obsessing over them. I knew this was toxic and that it would never end up how I wanted it; it had gone too far for that. I felt like I couldn't possibly move on or get over him in the same city, so I booked a one-way flight to America. I had to escape.

Two nights before I left, I posted a five-page letter to him as my closure. Projecting everything I felt, telling him I'd fallen in love with him but that I hated him so much. It was strange, though – by chance he had woken up at three o'clock and texted me saying he was really worried about me, without even knowing about the letter. But when he *had* read it, he didn't say a single word other than he wanted to see me for a coffee before I left.

I didn't want to meet him, but I couldn't refuse either. Before I went, I decided to change my hair colour. (If you know me, when anything happens between a guy and me, I dye my hair. It's my way of motivating change. You know, the whole "new hair, new you" bullshit.) He did a double-take when I arrived and said he barely recognised me and how much it suited me being dark. We had a coffee, and he forced a caramel shortbread down me because of how thin I looked to him. Still, not a single word was mentioned about the letter. We hugged and parted ways.

He was never mine, but losing him broke my heart.

~Unknown

And so off to America I went. I guess I was hoping to "find myself". I sunk a free bottle of white wine after taking my seat on the plane – I don't even drink white wine. Tears trickled down my face as I looked out of the window. I felt relief to be leaving him behind. Sun, sea and sand would be my new best friends.

Just three weeks after I arrived in America, he messaged me. He wanted to tell me he had a girlfriend… *a girlfriend*?! After everything he'd said: that he couldn't or didn't want to commit to me because he wanted to be single, that he didn't want a relationship. Then boom, I leave for the other side of the world and he suddenly gets a fucking girlfriend. Unfortunately for me, it was not a case of out of sight, out of mind. I was devastated, heartbroken to the core. There was nothing I could do or say, and those first two months were hell. I was trying to escape something, but it didn't matter where the fuck I was in the world – I just couldn't shake it.

I wish you knew how bad it fucked me up.

~Unknown

After six months in America I came back with even darker hair than when I left, feeling like a new woman, wild and free.

And within two weeks of being home, both of us single again, I was back in his bed.

I didn't have a car because I sold mine to go travelling, so I used to take my mum's in the middle of the night and make sure I was back by eight o'clock so she could go to work. I had slipped straight back into our fucked-up situation. It was like I'd never left. Only I pretended I was over him, that I didn't have feelings for him anymore, so it was safe to carry on. But who the fuck was I kidding? You can't just turn your feelings off for someone. I wish there was a switch, but there isn't.

This time it only lasted four months. I knew I couldn't continue this again. I didn't send an essay this time – no letter either, nothing. Instead, some gorgeous guy asked me out on a date and I said yes. And that's when the tables turned. Suddenly Max wanted me and wanted to make things work. But I was done. I couldn't take it anymore. I stuck to my guns and went on a date. Unfortunately, that didn't work out, but it was the perfect tonic. It helped me to realise that I could have a normal relationship and go on normal dates if I wanted to. I didn't need to torment myself by being Max's fuck toy any longer.

Funnily enough, not long after I was finally done with him was the night I bumped into Chris, and that was that. Fate stepped in, and within weeks, we were back together. Apart from seeing Max from afar on nights out, we barely said two words to each other for five years.

Soon we will be strangers. No, we can never be that. Hurting someone is an act of reluctant intimacy. We will be dangerous acquaintances with a history.

~Hanif Kureishi

In those five years, Max had four girlfriends. Not bad for a guy who didn't want a girlfriend, I thought. One of the saddest things about our relationship, though, aside from all the hurt, was that he was the reason I stopped writing. Before and during my time with him, I kept diaries and journals full of life and stories, but when I got back with Chris, I was petrified he would find them. Pages upon pages full of Max's name and explicit details of our wild sex life. I didn't want to be reminded of him anymore, so I put them all in a bin and set them alight. Watching the pages turn to ash was like a ritual cleansing of my soul, ridding me of a dirty past that had caused so much pain.

It took me a long time to fully get over Max. When I got back with Chris I was going out a lot less, but whenever I did go out I was always anxious that I would bump into Max. We frequented the same bars and we also had mutual friends, so it was inevitable, but my stomach still dropped every time he caught my eye. I remember when I got engaged, all I wanted to do was rub it in his face, though I quickly realised the man I was with was ten times the guy Max was ever going to be, and one day I stopped thinking about him.

When I look back now, I didn't love him. I was in love with the idea of him; of who I wanted him to be. I was infatuated, obsessed and in total lust with him. But I didn't love him.

If it's destroying you, then it isn't love, my dear.

~Unknown

I often wonder why there is that one guy that you always go back to. No matter how many times you say you're done and that you will never go back there, through the months, even years in this case, why do you always go back? Because it is a relationship that never really started but never really finished. It's unfinished business. I believe that's why.

Following the split with Chris, I went on an Instagram-following spree, and for some reason, Max came to mind. I wondered whether he still looked the same, where he was living, and what he was doing all these years on. It appeared he was in a happy relationship. Regardless of how he broke my heart, nothing but joy ran through my veins that he seemed to have finally settled down. However, it wasn't long before I saw his name appear in my direct messages. It turned out he was also going through a break-up. It was so strange; we started talking about how different our lives were to all those years ago. It was like offloading on to a long-lost friend with no other intention than catching up and being there for each other. He would pop up every now and then and ask how I was doing and fill me in with how his situation was going. He told me he felt like he was stuck and he didn't know what to do. Some nights we would discuss things for hours, and I would try and give him advice. I didn't have any urge to see him or put myself out there for him. I didn't even get excited about his messages. It almost felt like a form of therapy, bizarrely.

The weekend after my disastrous New Year's Eve, my friend Rose had our netball team over. It can get a little messy when we all get together for a sleepover. The youth comes out in us all, and we are like a group of teenagers, doing karaoke and trying to build human pyramids. It was just what I needed. But then the drinking games started. I'd had a rough few months, and okay, drinking probably wasn't the best idea, but I was with my girls in a safe environment.

The problem was, once I started drinking, I didn't want to stop. I never wanted the night to end. It helped to ease the pain of my sober reality. One by one, the girls started to drop off and settle down for the night, and it was then that I felt a sudden wave of sadness, and my anxiety kicked in at the thought of going to sleep. It was a proper sleepover club, all eight of us tucked up in our sleeping bags, spread out across the living room, but I couldn't get my mind to rest. I lay down as the others started to snore when *ping*, I got a message from Max. He was out and asked where I was. Barely able to string a sentence together, I must have made enough sense to have given him the indication I wanted to meet him.

Scared of being seen by anyone, he asked me to meet him down the road. Tip-toeing over everyone's limbs, trying to be as quiet as a mouse, I threw my coat over my white, silk pyjamas, put my slippers on and stumbled out the door. Not sure that's the outfit I would have planned to see the guy that broke my heart after five years, but there we go. It was so cold outside, my windows were all frozen, but even that didn't stop me. I got in my car, but before I'd even turned the ignition I saw my friend's husband running towards my car in his boxers and an oversized jumper. He leant straight into my car door and flung it open. "What the fuck are you doing?" He shouted. We began to argue, and I told him I was only going down the road. *Like that was OK.* After much persuasion, he got me into the house. If he hadn't, I dread to think what I could have done to myself or someone else. As I slowly walked back to the house with my head hung in shame, all the girls were stood by the door, looking at me with sheer disappointment. That very second, *that* was when I knew I had hit rock bottom.

Three of my closest friends were among the eight girls; Hannah, Chloe and Rose. The four of us headed into the kitchen. Chloe handed me a glass of water and told me to sit down. It was like an intervention. Worse, it was like I was getting told off at school by the strictest, most terrifying headteacher. But you know what? As much as I hated them all in that very second, it's what I needed. I needed them to be so brutally honest with me. I needed them to shout and scream at me. I told them I didn't want to be here, that Noah would be better off without me. Two of them even started to cry because they were so upset and concerned that I was fucking up my life right in front of their eyes.

After two hours my eyes couldn't take any more tears, so we decided to sleep. I messaged Max, apologising that I couldn't meet him and that was the last I heard from him, for now. The next morning, with what felt like the world's worst hangover, I knew something had to change.

I needed a detox from the world. The sad thing was that the first thing I thought about and needed to get rid of was social media. It was slowly killing me. I couldn't think straight while still comparing my life to everyone else's, feeling resentful towards the world, so I took three weeks out. I'm aware that doesn't sound a lot, but we have become so self-absorbed and obsessed with other people's lives, and without realising, our screen time on social media can quickly add up to a sickening amount of time. So, three weeks away made a world of difference. I didn't stop drinking completely. I still had the odd glass of wine, but I didn't go out. With my birthday coming up, I wanted to be in a better place mentally and to save a big night out of dancing and drinking until then. But can you really get yourself to a mentally healthier place in just three weeks? I thought I could…

I really don't give second chances; I give five or six.

Chapter Nine
The Disappointment

How to murder someone: kiss them once and never again.

~Unknown

I didn't want any more meaningless situations. I wanted more. I thought I was ready for more. With that in mind, I think I ruined this one before it even began. Overthinking, over-fantasising, overanalysing. I made it into something it wasn't and was never going to be. I didn't think I would get emotionally attached to someone so quickly. He was the first person I let myself get to know after breaking up with Chris and the first person I truly invested in. His name was Shane, the man that intentionally or not caused me so much pain. He was hilarious, but he also took me for a joke. I thought being Aaron and Ben's "other woman" was bad enough, but Shane showed me how easy it is to lose yourself when you're simply one of many.

Because we all eat lies when our hearts are hungry.

~Penelope Douglas

Following what happened on New Year's Eve, after taking some time away from men and social media, I was ready to face the world again. Returning to Instagram, I was greeted by numerous messages from Shane. There was something about him that caught my attention. Before him, I had only been with people I knew. I guess familiarity is comforting. Now here I was, with no idea about this man, and that made it so exciting. I had a look at our mutual friends (*I mean, who doesn't do that?*) and spotted Amy in his followers. Turns out, they had been good friends for years, and he had already messaged her about me. I was flattered, although little did I know then that I was merely one of many he had messaged Amy about. You might even say I was his next victim, but I'll let you be the judge of that...

In the beginning, Amy was all for the relationship. She told me how much he had grown up over the last few years and how different he was – apparently, he used to be wild and an outright player, cheating on girlfriends without a care in the world. But now, he wanted to find a woman and settle down. This gave me hope to think he wasn't around to fuck me over or just for a meaningless shag. He was maybe looking for something a little bit more, like I was.

He was so complimentary with everything. He told me how well I dressed, how unreal my body was, how I could never look terrible, that he should be thankful I even gave him a chance. It wasn't just about looks either. He gushed about how thoughtful I was, told me he really liked my personality and how different I was. Honestly, the list goes on. I know what you are thinking. *He just wanted to get into your pants*. But this is why it felt different. I can generally spot that if a man wants to see you within a week of speaking, then yes, he just wants to get into your pants, but Shane and I talked for seven weeks before we saw each other. You really get to know a person within seven weeks... Or so I thought.

During that time, I was up most nights until two o'clock talking to him, waking up to messages from him, and we would continue to speak for the majority of the next day. He was confident, which I found immensely attractive. He would pick up the phone and ring me. It freaked me out initially, as I wouldn't normally speak to someone on the phone if I hadn't met them yet. But with Shane, it became the norm. He had an accent that I had never heard before. It was very southern and almost a bit gangster-ish. It soon became a voice that I looked forward to hearing.

He loved his music as much as I do and said how remarkable my taste in music was, so we would send songs and videos to each other daily and listen to Instagram live videos together. He told me, "Listen to this artist, I think you'll really like them, " thinking he knew my taste down to a T already. He was, at this point, quite literally music to my ears. Looking back, this was obviously so normal to Shane, but to me, it was so rare. I had only had that with Max previously, but it was still different. It felt more personal. Music is such a massive part of my life, and I loved being able to share that interest with someone. Shane, on the other hand, was probably forwarding those songs to ten other women… but I'll get to that later.

Fuck nudes, send me your playlist.

~Unknown

His job required him to travel all around Europe, and for some women, this would be their worst nightmare, not knowing when you're going to see someone. For me, it was perfect. I live a very busy life, being a full-time mum and running my own business, although this didn't stop me from thinking about the future. Rightly or wrongly, I wondered where it could go, what we could become, how things might work out. I think it's only natural to think of these things when you are a mum. After all, I will never be able to give my full attention to anyone anymore. Noah is my main priority, and I have to think about the right person fitting in around him. I need someone who is as relaxed as me and not too eager to see me all the time.

Our relationship got quite intense quickly, with him asking me to catch the next flight to where he was working. He was full of ideas. He said we should go see my favourite artist in concert and see shows in London together. We should visit places like Liverpool, where parts of my family live, or go to Dublin for the weekend and get drunk together. It was *him,*

him, him. I would have never said those things because I didn't want to look too keen, but that is the thing with words, women (i.e. me) run a mile with them. But I still couldn't believe it hadn't fizzled out yet. I get bored so quickly with people, and I get turned off very easily, too (literally the slightest thing like putting a kiss on every message or calling me baby, eurgh). But when he called me baby girl, it was a different story.

We never ran out of things to say to each other. God, he was funny, he made me laugh more and more each day, and before him I had forgotten what it felt like to go to sleep and look forward to speaking to someone the next day. He was always telling me what to watch next on Netflix; he knew my heart belonged to horrors and that I loved to be scared, so he would send me videos to wake up to that would scare the living shit out of me. Of course, I freakishly loved that. We sent each other pictures of films we would watch and play "guess the film", as our competitive sides matched. You will know by now that I am all for a connection. I cannot just entertain someone for the sake of it or because they are good looking, have a fancy job title or have money – none of those things has ever mattered to me. I had not felt anything like this for a long time. Apart from Chris, the last person I had felt that connected to was Max.

Something about you made me feel a little more alive and far less lost.

~The Better Man Project

"You don't know it yet, but I'm taking you out, " was one of the first things Shane ever said to me. Within four or five weeks of talking, our conversations became very sexualised, and maybe this is where I went wrong. I had never sent anyone that I hadn't met before a picture of myself, but I strangely trusted him. He, of course, sent pictures too (he actually sent more graphic ones than me) but said, "I'm really not like that usually, " which made me trust him even more. He told me that he wasn't a "shagger" these days and that he couldn't remember the last time he'd had sex. I remember thinking, *My God, where has this man been hiding?* Now I just think, *you gullible twat, Elle.* I remember wondering whether I was ever actually going to see this man or whether we were just going to have this weird sexting, phone sex, text-ationship. I kept thinking, why has he not asked to see me yet? Is this just what he does? Or does he like me enough to not want to rush things?

As the weeks went on, I started becoming more and more fond of him. I went to visit Amy in Newcastle one weekend, and as we were out, she received a text message from him saying: *How's my girl? I hope you're looking after her for me.* It was still all him. He would ask me again and again how to get into my "top three" spot and that he wanted to reach number one. I would say he was slowly getting up there but would have to keep on grafting, to which he would reply that he would do anything until he was at the top. I once sent him a picture of an old married couple in the gym who looked so in love to which he replied: "I want to get to that with you." I will give it to him; his grafting game was strong.

We had in-depth conversations about our pasts and our exes, and he told me he wanted to get married one day. He rang me one evening after he had been to see his friends that had children, all excited about how amazing they were, how he loved it and that it made him really want kids of his own. I never got embarrassed talking about Noah either with him. I loved how much he would ask and talk about him. It felt so natural to be completely myself with him. I never wanted to lie to him. It wasn't long before he revealed that he still lived at home, and I thought *that's why he's not asked to see me or to go round his.* So, I finally bit the bullet and asked him to come over to mine. This again is where I went wrong. I wanted him to take me out, to go out on a date, but by inviting him over, it automatically turned into something I didn't want it to be. I was just sick of waiting for him, so I plucked up the courage when I was drunk and asked him instead. It came to Sunday, the day I was supposed to see him, and I hadn't heard from him all day. I thought, here we go. I text to say: *Bailing on tonight then?*

You were drunk. I didn't think you were serious. I'm in London, steaming.

I don't do second chances! I fired back. And that's when the messages flooded in…

Pleaseeeeeeee, I beg you.

Baby girl, please, I want you.

I'm sorry.

Little did he know at this point – I really don't give second chances; I give five or six.

I left him to it for two days. If he wanted to see me, he would. Lo and behold, by Tuesday in came the messages and phone calls, telling me how much he wanted to meet up. I couldn't just fall at his feet and be at his beck and call, so I played it cool. By cool, I mean I left it a massive *one* day before the night came where I first got to meet him (I know, not cool). When he told me he was en route, I necked two glasses of wine for some courage. I was so nervous I didn't know what to do with myself. I went for the casual, effortless look by doing my hair and makeup but throwing on some little grey shorts with a matching baggy jumper. However, what was underneath was very thought out, with matching black lace lingerie. I still remember his face as he turned up at my front door. The confident man I thought he was seemed so shy. As he walked in, he looked me up and down, and I could have ripped his clothes off that very second, but instead, he followed me into the lounge and didn't sit down until I said: "You can sit down, you know."

It didn't take long for his confident side to come out, grabbing his chance to sit next to me by showing me something on his phone. He went straight into talking about how much he really wanted kids, which was the second time he had said that to me in a week. But ten minutes later, the conversation came to a sudden halt when his phone buzzed and flashed up *ALEX CALLING*. He quickly brushed it off: "It's my mate. I really can't be bothered to speak to him right now." Alarm bells were ringing, but I chose not to say anything. After all, I had only just met the guy.

After talking and laughing for a while, we put on one of his favourite films. Snuggled up on the sofa, I felt so comfortable with him, my legs sprawled across his waist as he didn't stop massaging and tickling me. About half an hour into the film, the butterflies in my stomach (or should I say my pants) were doing somersaults, and I couldn't take it any longer. His hands got higher and higher, and I knew I couldn't resist his touch, so I grabbed his hand and squeezed it tight to indicate I wanted him. I wanted him so badly. He immediately turned around and started to kiss me. His lips were perfect. I could instantly tell how wet I was as his hands went down on me, pushing my pants to the side. He began to say how amazing my pussy was and how good I was at kissing. My hands moved from the nape of his neck to gripping his muscly back as his fingers started off slow and gentle. His whole body was soon touching mine, with just our clothes between us. I could feel how hard he was pressed up against my legs as his fingers went deeper and deeper. I pushed him to sit upright and swung my legs across his waist. He wriggled down his tracksuit bottoms, leaving his red Calvin Kleins on so I could feel his hardness even more. Grinding my hips on him, he slowly undressed me, touching my whole body, kissing my breasts as he unclipped my bra.

Biting my lip as I moaned into his mouth, his fingers re-entered me, penetrating more and more. This is the part where I would have liked to say I pulled away, to not come across as easy, to be more of a challenge. But I wanted sex. I wanted him inside me. Both already sweating and panting like dogs, his Calvins and t-shirt were no longer to be seen. He grabbed my body, lifting it up; replacing me so I was lying on my back. Towering over me, he moaned, "You're so tight, " as he entered me. He felt so good inside of me, but then he would stop, grab my thighs and spread them apart and kept going down on me to make him last longer.

He flipped me over so my face was pressed hard against the armrest, his hands going from round my neck to pulling my hair as he got rougher and quicker with every thrust. Then again going down on me from behind, making me even wetter. We were in every position – cushions flying everywhere, my moans getting more and more aggressive by the second. He then pulled me up against the corner of the sofa and placed his fingers back inside me. I felt like I was going to explode. As I yelled, "Don't stop, please don't stop, " he got quicker and deeper, and then I exploded, squirting all over his hands. Surprisingly, it took longer than usual because I was nervous, and I had to really think about relaxing my body, but when it came, it *came*. My legs shaking from my eruption, I wanted him instantly inside of me again. Rock hard, he put himself back into me, my inner thighs drenched, rubbing against his, each thrust getting harder and deeper. My hands went from his wet clean-shaven chest quickly to the back of his neck, pulling him in closer, moaning into his ear as his breath got shorter and shorter. He let out a huge roar as he came inside of me, to which I moaned, "Oh my God, *yes*, " as my legs began to twitch. I could have gone again and again all night.

Not long after we got our breath back, rummaging around the room for our underwear and laughing about how we had both left our socks on, like clockwork the tickling was straight back on, he even started massaging my head and playing with my hair as I laid my head on his legs. I felt so satisfied and content. I sometimes feel a bit awkward after sex, particularly if the guy doesn't want to cuddle. Why, oh, why do woman get so emotionally attached after sex? I know it is scientifically proven that women release the "cuddle hormone" while men are programmed to detach after sex, but Shane did the opposite.

He began an in-depth conversation about his family and the battles they've been through. I have always struggled to keep eye contact with most people, but as I turned my head towards his face, I couldn't take my eyes off him as he was telling me something that seemed so deep and personal. We carried on watching the rest of the film, but within just minutes, he blurted out: "I want to be honest with you, I really don't want to lie to you, " I thought, *please not today Satan, please.* Much to my surprise, he said: "That was a girl that rang me earlier, I've been trying to shake her off for weeks, but she hasn't got the hint." He continued to say he had never met her. He had just matched with her on a dating app, but she was desperate, and he wasn't interested.

Looking back now, I wish I had kicked him out there and then, but I felt like I couldn't say anything – we weren't dating, and for all he knew, I was talking to other people as well. So, I instead took him at face value. I took it as him wanting to be honest with me, and actually, I really respected him for that. My God, that "cuddle hormone" fucks us over every time and makes our judgement extremely cloudy.

One thing I learned a long time ago was to never ignore the red flags in the beginning, or they'll be the same reason it all ends.

~M. Sosa

I hadn't had someone touch me that way in so long. With other men, it was just sex, no build-up of getting to know one another, no feelings. As he went to leave, we stood at the door for twenty minutes, kissing like teenagers. As I was wrapped up in his arms, I could feel my word vomit coming up… "I've had a C-section, that's why I have a big scar across my stomach. Just saying."

He looked me right in the eyes, pulled me in closer and replied, "As if I even care about that, " and kissed me on my forehead. *Killer.* Just before he left, he grabbed my legs with both hands, picked me up with my legs wrapped tightly around his waist, and he kissed me even more. This man right here was sweeping me off my feet. When he left, I was shocked to see within just a few minutes his number appear on my phone and he spoke to me his whole journey home, he told me how amazing I looked in real life, even better than photos and that he really enjoyed himself and he couldn't wait to see me again. *Wow.* You know what they say, the devil is, and always will be, a gentleman!

He gave her the thing that she wanted the most. He made her feel desired.

~Unknown

In my experience, a few days later is where it can go one way or the other – they've either got what they wanted, and all of a sudden, their attitude towards you changes, or they seem more invested than ever because they want to see you again. Shane couldn't have reacted better. I joked to him about not wanting to put all my eggs in one basket because of Alex, to which he replied, "She's got the hint. You're mine. You're my only piece, Elle. I don't want to play games." He seemed keener than ever, and it made me feel so secure. He made me feel like I was the only person he was interested in. I wouldn't say I was falling for this guy. I was just falling for his tricks because, unfortunately, I hadn't yet realised that the language he was, in fact speaking, was straight out of the fuckboy dictionary. My God, he knew what he was doing.

Within days he wanted to see me again, but our schedules clashed as I had Noah. That weekend, just four days after our night together, he rang me to drop a bombshell: he had just found out that he had to work in Germany for eight weeks and was leaving in the morning. My heart slumped as I thought, *typical.* He told me not to worry, that things wouldn't change between us, that he wanted to see where things would go and see me as soon as he got back.

I couldn't help think that he must have known about the trip before then. *He obviously just wanted to get his end away before his trip.* But then I found myself giving him the benefit of the doubt and allowing him to tug on my heart strings. If we didn't see each other for seven weeks before then, we would be able to do another eight weeks if he was into this. Having finally met someone that I really liked and then not knowing when I would see him again really took its toll, though. Yes, distance makes the heart grow fonder, but it can turn you into a crazy motherfucker too. Maybe it was a blessing in disguise, maybe if he didn't go away, we would have seen each other more, and I would have been even more emotionally attached to him. Maybe I'd have fallen in love and had my heart broken. *Maybe.*

As far as my luck goes, it seems that when it rains, it pours, and a week after Shane left, I found out that my two assistant hairdressers had been poaching my clients for their new salon. It took a toll on my mental health to see everything I had built up for the last two years was about to crash and burn right in front of my eyes.

I felt betrayed and cheated, but as they knew I only worked part-time because of Noah, they agreed to work a month's notice. As much as I wanted to fire both the snakes on the spot, to tell them to "Sod your months' notice, pack your hairdryers and go, " I couldn't, because I couldn't run the salon and look after Noah without them.

They say bad things come in threes, right? The same week of my assistant crisis, I had my dreaded hospital letter about my pre-operation assessment. I'd had an ongoing problem with my stomach since having Noah that had caused me numerous hospital trips in agony over the last few years. It was suspected endometriosis, and the second I got the letter, I found myself panicking that I might never have children again. It was well and truly pouring rain in every aspect of my life.

I felt tears building up every day as my mind constantly felt elsewhere. I couldn't bear to look my two assistants in the face. I took a step away from the salon to figure out my next steps, and suddenly I had all this free time to think and reflect. Feelings and emotions from the past year seemed to creep back up, so I decided to get it all out, write everything down and hey, who knows, maybe one day it would turn into a book. I told Shane that I had started to write a book, but that I didn't know what I would do with it. He asked about it most days and seemed to really care about it, telling me how amazing he thought it was that I was doing it and that he knew an editor if I ever wanted to get my work published.

Aside from a couple of friends, he was the only other person that knew what I was writing. I trusted him a lot, and the more I started to write, the more I opened up to the idea of one day sharing my story with the world. I divulged my hopes and dreams, worries, and fears with Shane and spoke at length about how the book might be received by people who knew me. He would settle my mind by telling me about critique and how to learn to live with it. We even joked about what he wanted to be called in my book and whether he would be the longest or shortest chapter. He once said, "Whether it is the longest or the shortest, it will be the best." He made me feel like he was different, so different from all my other chapters. And he *was* different. He was not like all the previous chapters – he was so much worse.

The more days I spent away from the salon, the more social anxiety I got and the more I felt like I didn't want to return. Not knowing when I would return or if I could ever pick the salon up again, my mind started drifting into a negative state. And having time to evaluate my feelings and overthink every last detail of Shane and I did me no favours. A situation that should have been so simple very quickly became incredibly complex, not to mention intense and deep. I've always worn my heart on my sleeve. I've always sent reckless texts to people confessing my feelings for them, hitting send then throwing my phone, pretending I don't want a reply from them when really that's all I want. This is my problem – I overthink, and I feel too deeply. I don't know how to rest my mind. I am continually questioning, searching for the meaning of everything. I cannot control my emotions. I have never been able to.

Within three weeks of Shane leaving for Germany, his true colours began to show. He began to blow hot and cold with me, and the man I thought was so honest soon had me doubting his every word. It started off with little things like saying goodnight to me at two o'clock in the morning but staying online for another hour or so. I mean, men aren't even letting us be psychos and FBI agents these days; they are shoving it right in our faces, clear as day to see with their WhatsApp "last seen" status. They just do not give a fuck. He would ring me and I would, of course, pick up, but whenever I rang him, he wouldn't answer. He would say he was busy or working or sometimes wouldn't even acknowledge that I called him. Everything seemed to be on his terms. As he was away from home, he told me about an app that allowed him to keep in contact with everyone from home in a different way. It was similar to Facetime, except it allowed video chatting and playing games with multiple people on the screen at one time, and you could also see who was talking to who. It was this app that signalled the beginning of the end.

At first, he would be on the app with just me, and it seemed like a fun new way to keep in touch. But as the days went by, I started to see that nearly every night, Shane was using the app with a different woman. Now, don't get me wrong, I wouldn't usually have a problem with this. I have plenty of male friends, but my problem was that whenever I went online, within seconds, he would change his status to being in a locked conversation which meant I could no longer see who he was talking to. *Shady as fuck.*

I want you so badly.
But I don't want this.

~L. E. Bowman

It wasn't long before we had our first argument. In these situations, you have to weigh up your options – do you hang on and give someone the power to hurt you further down the line, or do you grab control and walk away from the situation but always wonder what could have been? Deep down, it's not what I wanted at all, but I guess it doesn't hurt as much if you are the one who leaves – at least that way, you save face. I could feel my blast from the past blubbering up, and, just as I had done with Max, I sent him a text expressing my feelings. They had such similarities to each other it was scary. I was terrified of slipping into another toxic situation, so I tried to push him away. I've always pushed the people I want in my life away. I threaten to leave because, deep down, all I want is someone to tell me how stupid I am being and to tell me I'm worth not giving up. You know, to just try.

I childishly made a few digs about the app and told him that I wanted him to be honest with me. I told him that if he wanted to fuck around, I didn't want to be one of many and would leave him to it. He told me he was disappointed in my message and that he was scared at the thought of me trying to control him. I wondered if I had overreacted so I apologised, blaming my behaviour on overthinking. He told me to not worry about it, and just like that, we carried on speaking normally, as if nothing had happened.

Only it wasn't back to normal. Over the next five weeks it was a rollercoaster of emotions, and he ended up consuming my every waking mood. If he spoke to me in the morning, I was on cloud nine, and if he didn't, I would spend the whole day waiting to hear from him. I felt utterly obsessed with this text-ationship. Well, I was more like a fucking pen pal now. Even my friends started to notice. They'd ask: "What's up with you, has Shane not spoken to you today?" They'd tell me to just ghost him and forget about him, but I couldn't.

Day by day, my anxiety worsened as I sat dwelling over how someone could change so quickly. I lost half a stone in two weeks. Of course, he wasn't the only reason. I still couldn't face returning to the salon, then the flip side of that was the money stress of being out of work, as well as the worry of when my operation would be and what the results would be – there was so much more to it, Shane was just the cherry on top. But I knew at this point that I had grown extremely attached to him, and that it wasn't going to end well.

You deserve something you don't have to question. You deserve someone who is sure about you.

~R.H. Sin

With Shane knowing my current struggles with my business, he would continuously ask me if I was okay. If I was having a bad day, he would reassure me and later ask if I was feeling better and tell me everything would work out. When the date arrived for my pre-operative assessment, he made sure he checked in with me just before and didn't leave it an hour before he messaged again, asking if I was okay and how it all went. He had bad days, too, telling me how much he missed home and how he was worried whether his family would be coping without him, so we would try and cheer each other up, but as the weeks went on, he seemed to be getting used to this new life, and I was getting worse. It wasn't long until our second argument.

One afternoon Shane said he had something funny to tell me and send me screenshots of his conversations with the same girl who had called when he was at my house, Alex. From what I could see, she had been sending him messages, but he wasn't replying. I was so confused. Why was he showing me texts from a woman he said he shook off six weeks ago? He really thought I would believe that she was still messaging him? No. I was sure he must have still been entertaining the poor woman, probably telling her precisely what she wanted to hear. It didn't add up nor sit well with me.

Again, I couldn't hold back, so I expressed how confused I felt by his apparent lies. Straight away, he turned it around on me, accusing me of using his honesty against him, telling me that he had been truthful and that I wanted to believe what I chose to. This is where my walls came crashing down. I laid my feelings on the table. I told him that if I liked him now, imagine how I would feel in another three months. I told him I really didn't want to get hurt. After what felt like forever, he finally claimed, "I obviously like you too." He also said he didn't want us to stop speaking and understood why I needed to express my feelings. However, he also took the opportunity to tell me that he couldn't promise we would ever end up in a relationship. That was a game-changer. It was never about that. I was never asking for that level of commitment. I was asking that he didn't hurt me, but it seems I was simply asking the wrong person – because that is exactly what he did.

Despite the arguments, Shane still had me hooked. One minute he would say that my house would be his first stop the second his plane landed and joke around that he's "found the one" with me. But then the next minute he wouldn't speak to me for two days. It wasn't that long ago he was asking me to catch a flight out to see him, but that no longer seemed an option. I felt utterly obsessed with him, fantasising about getting the next flight out to Germany. He would continuingly tell me he had nothing to do in his hotel room after work, so why the fuck was he online all the time and not speaking to me?! When we did speak on the phone, he would end the call by saying he was going to watch TV, but then seconds after hanging up he'd go straight onto the app. My head was scrambled. He was lying to me, and I had no idea why. Every day I battled with the same questions: *Why hasn't he spoken to me today? Why hasn't he replied to me when he's been online? Has he found someone better? Is he bored of me? Am I not pretty enough? Is it because I'm a mum?* It was emotionally and physically draining me.

When you were little and played on the beach, you knew that one red flag in the water meant danger. Hazard. Be Careful. Stay Cautious. When you were little and played on the beach, you knew that two red flags meant kid, get out of the fucking water. Now. The beach is closed. Go home. And yet, here he is, showing more red flags than your younger self could ever count, so tell me, why are you still paddling at his feet?

~SRWPOETRY

Shane's placement in Germany was extended for four weeks, and after ten weeks, I no longer understood who he was at all. Each time I expressed my feelings and told him I couldn't do this anymore, he would manipulate me into thinking I was being petty, fishing for an argument, that it was my fault, and somehow I would end up apologising every time. He was gaslighting me, and I couldn't see through all the haze. It was at this point that I realised I was fucked, and there was no return. I had let down my walls. I had told him so much about myself, my hopes, dreams, past, and fears. He knew *me.* But I wanted it all back. He didn't deserve to know all those things. It made me so vulnerable; he knew exactly how I felt about him, and as soon as you let that go, you can't take it back. Whether they intentionally mean to or not, they then take advantage of knowing how you feel and have got you eating out their palm of their hands.

Alex got brought up a third and final time when I saw her starting to watch my Instagram stories. I asked Shane if she knew about me, and he said no, that she must have been going through his followers and stalking all the women. If this woman was this invested in him without even meeting him, can you imagine how much I was? It turned into another argument, and my head went from scrambled to fried. Were my insecurities taking full control over my mind and making me think the worst of everything, or was this man just playing me like a goddamn fool?

If you feel like you are being played, you probably are.

~NCIS

I talked to Amy and she knew how much of a hit my mental health was taking, so she got in her car and started the four-hour drive from Newcastle to stay with me for the week. There was a lot of wine and cuddles – just what I needed from my best friend. Despite being Shane's friend, she admitted that she had seen a different side to him. "Bin him off. He's not worth it, " she told me. And she was right, he wasn't worth it. I was looking for happiness in someone that was effectively taking it away. The situation had already fucked me up, so I wrote what I thought was one last message to him and walked away (metaphorically, at least). I asked him not to reply, and he respected what I wanted and didn't. Unfortunately, the story doesn't end here.

Amy left to go back home, and after just two days silly old me got drunk, and in a moment of weakness, I texted him. *WHY DO I DO THIS?* It was then that I became my own worst enemy. I became desperate. I became desperate to change his opinion of me; desperate for an explanation and answers, even though they weren't things he owed to me. We weren't together. You're allowed to change your mind, you're allowed to not want anything to do with a person anymore, but I've never been able to accept that. I just can't let shit go. I always thought I would rather someone be as hurtful as they can towards me so I can hate them and move on.

For two weeks we went back and forth, going around in circles, going back over the same rows we'd had previously. I mean, I was having relationship problems with someone I wasn't in a relationship with. It was fucked.

Shane was patronising, asking if I had been drinking again. His replies got later and later, and I was getting more and more wound up and frustrated waiting around for him. He said that he was disappointed it was ending like this. It was the second time he had said he was disappointed in me. But I knew that actually, he was the only disappointment. His behaviour over the last few weeks had opened my eyes, and I realised he was not someone I would ever want to be with. So why was I doing it to myself? What was I holding on to?

I don't know why we all hang on to something we know we're better off letting go of. It's like we are scared to lose what we don't really have.

~Meredith Grey

Shane's twelve weeks of working away were up, and I didn't even know if he was back home or still in Germany. I just knew that I still wanted answers. I begged for honesty, and better late than never, he finally handed it to me on a silver platter. He was never ever going to tell me what I wanted to hear. He was never going to give me what I wanted. He told me that he didn't want to commit to one person, he wanted the freedom to speak to other people and sleep with other people, and he didn't think that would be something I would agree to. *What a fucking prick.* For starters, what woman in their right mind would be OK with that after all the things he said? He sucked me right in to just spit me straight back out. If that were the vibe I had got from the start, before there were feelings, then maybe it could have been a casual thing, just sex, like it was with Aaron and Ben. He wanted me until something better came along. He wasn't the man I knew months ago; he was a fucking fraud.

It was never about commitment, though. I never asked him to commit to me. For God's sake, I had met the man once. It was such a natural thing for me to stop talking to other men because I liked him, but that's not to say I wanted a relationship with him. For me, it's simple – why would I entertain other guys when I'm happily entertained by this one? I had other options I could have explored, but I didn't because I didn't want to.

I think we can carry on talking, just not as much as we were, was his later reply.

Was this man taking the absolute piss out of me? He wanted to put a time limit on how much we talked from then on. No. I was not going to be this man's puppet any longer. He had controlled everything for the past three months. I wasn't having him control when I could and couldn't speak to him.

It was a wicked game you played with my heart. Pulling on strings as though I were your puppet and you the master.

~Makenzie Campbell

I regret that we weren't able to leave the situation without bitterness. I told Shane that he was a dick and a waste of my time. *Ouch,* but true. He fired back, saying that he never promised me anything. True, but why say things in the first place if you don't mean them? Why call me "your girl" when in actual fact, I wasn't and was never going to be? I never have and never will understand that. He said that I was too intense, over the top and that I gave him stress. But at the end of the day, my behaviour was a reflection of how he was treating me. I had stupidly got attached, and for what? I was left feeling alone and not good enough because I was the idiot who put all her eggs in one basket.

I know I worry too much about what people think of me; I always have done, and I worried about what he thought of me. I worried and cared about his aspirations, his family and their complications, his life, anything he shared with me. I cared because that is the type of person I am. But when it all comes crashing down, what do you do with all this information? Are you just supposed to forget about it? That's hard for me. As I said earlier, I remember the important stuff. And I don't just remember it, I care about it. I guess that's why I'm so vulnerable to getting hurt – I trust people's words instead of believing their actions.

Really this was his loss. And I don't mean that in a sassy, *oh well, his loss* kind-of-way. It was his loss because while I lost someone who didn't give a damn about me, he lost someone who really did care about him.

I have such a fucking big heart that I always see the good in people. I always judge people on how they treat me – not based on other people's opinions. I got told to be careful with him – "this one has commitment issues" and "he sleeps with everyone, " but I chose to listen to HIS words. I mean, don't get me wrong, I didn't start speaking to this man thinking I would marry him. I was just ready to meet someone that could potentially be something a little more than just sex. I don't think it's a bad trait to always see the good in people, I would never want to change that about myself, but it just means you have to be prepared for people to disappoint you.

I still struggle to understand why you would fill women with bullshit if you don't mean it. For what? Just for sex? For attention? To fill a void? To just feel wanted? God, he must do it to hundreds of women, and I was *so* angry with myself for letting him do that to me. Every day I would check the new women he was following on Instagram, comparing myself to them: she's younger than me, she's skinnier than me, she's got bigger tits than me, she's a model, she's Irish, he will love that. I don't know why we put ourselves through it. I was so angry that he made a fool out of me. I was so angry that all this time, I thought I was special, when in reality he was more than likely saying the same things to ten other women. I was so angry that I trusted him and sent pictures of my body when he probably received similar images from different women every day. Christ, he's probably got a whole folder full of them.

You are more than enough to hold someone's attention, don't settle for anyone who tried to come to you with theirs divided.

~Butterflies Rising

I think I will always wonder why with him. Why did he want me so bad in the beginning then not want me at all? Why did he change his mind? Why wasn't I good enough? It's the feeling of being so replaceable and so forgettable. The pain of not feeling good enough has got to be one of the worst pains to endure. It is like these men want you, but the second they see your insecurities and imperfections, they don't want you anymore. He saw my soft side, the real me and disregarded it. The scars go deeper each time a man makes you feel like you're not good enough. You don't have to fall in love with people or date someone for them to hurt you, the pain has no limits, and it all feels the same.

Looking back, I probably didn't know what I wanted, but I wanted him so much more when he didn't want me. *Shock.*

And while I might not know exactly what I want, I now know what kind of man I don't want, and that is a man like Shane.

He will never know how much I cried over it. He consumed five months of my life, five fucking months on a guy I met just once! It's ludicrous, fucking batshit crazy. I was trapped in a text-ationship, and I felt like I couldn't get out. He still feels like such a big part of my single life, and I do wonder how someone you have only met once can be such a significant chapter, yet, in reality, he really is just a few pages. I was probably just a flicker in his life, and he won't even remember my name in a year, but I won't be able to forget him and the way he made me feel.

For weeks on end, even though I knew walking away from the situation was the right thing to do, every time my phone went I hoped it was him. Every time there was a knock at the door, I thought it would be him or at least some flowers, apologising, saying he messed up and admitting he'd let a good one go. Asking for that second chance that he so desperately wanted in the beginning. And that's me. Even after he's shown his true colours and revealed every single sign of being a fuck boy, I still think about all the good in him, or maybe the good I thought he was. I just hope I never hear from him again.

I pulled myself up off the floor and flung myself onto my bed. I wailed into my pillow for over an hour, and for the first time in an exceptionally long time, I reached out to God.

Chapter Ten
The Heartbreaker – Continued

You're not a bad person for the ways you tried to kill your sadness.

~Hannah Elizabeth Francis

When things ended with Shane, I felt so meaningless and low, the only thing I knew to do was to get attention elsewhere. You know, the whole "you have to get under someone to get over someone" bullshit. Is seeing the person that shattered my heart and sleeping with them a good idea? No. But did I do it anyway? Of course I did. I go back to what I know and what I deem to be easy, again and again.

Max replied to one of my Instagram stories a couple of nights after Shane and I finished things, and within twenty minutes of replying, he was in my house. It felt so different from years ago. I could openly talk to him about how he broke my heart, and we could laugh about it. Weird, right? We also laughed about the five-page letter I wrote to him. He told me how fucked he was with alcohol and drug abuse when we were together and that he couldn't remember a lot of it and that he would change it if he could, but everything happens for a reason. *Boy, don't I know it.*

We talked over a few beers for what felt like hours. At one point, I thought we weren't even going to sleep with each other. There was no flirting, no sexual reference to anything. It was like we were just two good friends having a catch-up. But as he went to leave, the tables turned very quickly, and we were upstairs in bed in a flash.

For the first time ever we kissed, we kissed a lot. The most bizarre thing is, I would have given anything for that years ago, but it didn't make my tummy flutter or my heart jump like I thought it would. There was no foreplay, no warm-up, just straight to it. He undid his belt and pulled down his trousers as he lay on his back, a well-recognized image. I straddled him as we both took our own tops off, grinding my hips on his familiar body. But my body was so different to all those years ago. He groped my breasts that I didn't have before as I got quicker and quicker, and then he told me to turn around so he could see my ass fucking him. The faster I went, the more he moaned and smacked my ass, just like he used to. We flipped over, my hands grabbing the top of my headboard and my back arched, ready for him to enter me again. "I'm going to come in seconds fucking you like that, " he moaned and after a few thrusts from behind, he started to twitch, and it was all over.

It wasn't you I was kissing–don't be mistaken.
It was him on my mind, your lips were just convenient.

~Rupi Kaur

It was very average sex compared to the crazy nights of our past. Probably a lot more exciting than some people's sex lives, but still. It was almost like we had done absolutely everything in the book previously, and there was nothing new to explore. It will always be good sex with him, but the passion was gone. It didn't make me scream and beg for more as I had before. I remember thinking all those years ago, how will I ever get over this man? And here I was, wishing that the man I was once so besotted with was someone else. And there is something so liberating about that.

I wanted sex to help me forget about Shane, and it did everything but. After we got dressed, he made his way to the door, and we kissed goodbye. Seconds after the door shut, it was as if my body was about to shut down. I fell to the ground like a dead weight, and tears came streaming down my face. "Why do I keep doing this to myself?" I shrieked. I felt emptier than ever. I felt hollow. I felt more alone and unwanted than I did before. I pulled myself up off the floor and flung myself onto my bed. I wailed into my pillow for over an hour, and for the first time in an exceptionally long time, I reached out to God.

I cannot remember the last time I cried out to God. When I think about it, was I crying out to God? Do I even believe in God? I don't know, but I know I was reaching out to someone, looking for someone to hear me, for someone to save me from all the heartache I had consumed over the past year. It wasn't just Shane I was crying over; I felt the overwhelming feeling that I had lost myself again, exactly how I felt after breaking up with Chris. I was back at square one, where I was so desperately asking for the meaning of life and what the purpose of all this hurt was.

Everything I had been through, all these men I had been with, shattered my soul. One by one, they had taken parts from me, and it had left me empty.

Chapter Eleven
The Turning Point

It's not always just the heart. Sometimes your mind breaks as well.

~R.H. Sin

I was on a downward spiral after my night with Max. Unfortunately, that wasn't my wake-up call. I needed to feel even emptier. I needed to hit rock bottom, deeper than ever before. Whenever Noah was with Chris, I couldn't bear being alone. The second I dropped him off, I would go to Lucy's or my mum's, or whoever would have me. I hated the thought of being on my own.

A couple of weeks after sleeping with Max, I went out for dinner and a couple of beers with Liam. We sat in his garden until it started to get chilly, chatting about anything and everything. I spoke about Shane, but I sugar-coated how it had really made me feel. We talked about me being a single mum and all its complications. Bless him, he knew exactly the right thing to say. He was so supportive. He made me feel at ease, explaining that it would make no difference to him if he met someone that had a child. That I was in such a good position because my ex and I get on and that the only thing that would scare him away as if there was hostility between us. We even talked about the moon and the stars. Deep, right? At no point was there any flirtatious behaviour or mixed signals between us. He really is amazing, and such a good friend. I made myself a cup of tea as we moved inside to sit on separate sofas and watch a horror film. Yawning away, I decided to make a move home, thanking him for a lovely evening as we hugged and parted ways.

A few days later, Lucy had a BBQ that we were both invited to, along with my best friend again… alcohol. From the moment I got there, I couldn't wait to crack open a bottle of prosecco. It was four o'clock when I took my first sip in the thirty-degree English heat. Never without a drink in my hand; never without chain-smoking and dancing the night away. When you are drinking and dancing, everything just seems so far away; everything that you are going through feels so distant for just a little while. The night was running away with me, and before I knew it, it was close to midnight and I was wasted.

She remained drunk to cloak her fear of never being good enough.

~Christopher Poindexter

We made our way into the house, where waves of sickness soon overtook me. I've only been sick from alcohol a few times in my life, and this was one of them. Hurling all my prosecco back up into the toilet, tears streamed down my face. I hate being sick so much. You know when you just want your mum? I slumped back on the sofa next to Liam, where he began to comfort me.

I felt comfortable and safe around him, but I couldn't shake off feeling hopelessly sorry for myself, and the next thing I knew I was texting Shane and telling him he was a "head fuck" because he liked my picture on Instagram that evening. I begged him to block me. Piteous, I know, it was just a photo, but I was still holding on to anything. He read it, and there was no reply. Twenty minutes later, when Lucy asked where we were staying, I quickly told her, "Liam and I will sleep in the spare room" – I wanted cuddles.

As I climbed into bed, we started to cuddle. But the feeling of embarrassment and rejection wouldn't leave my body, so I came on to Liam. I had absolutely zero self-control. Someone shows me a little bit of attention, and I run with it. Can you see a pattern here? I had been sick for God's sake; I was a complete and total mess. He probably only kissed me back because he felt sorry for me.

I didn't feel anything. I was half porn star, half-dead weight. My head was spinning; I was thinking that I was either going to throw up again or pass out. *What the fuck am I doing?* I thought. *Why am I actually having sex right now?* I knew it wasn't going to magically make me feel better.

Halfway through, I told him we needed to stop. Of course, he immediately did and began to cuddle me, making sure I was okay. I claimed tiredness and needing sleep. This guy really gets the worst of me, and he, of all people, doesn't deserve that. It wasn't anything he did; I just realised that my reason for sleeping with him was unfair. I know people use people for sex all the time, but I didn't want to use him to try and get over someone else. He didn't deserve to get the drunk me. Granted, I might act like a porn star, but I'm doing it for all the wrong reasons. The thing is, he didn't have a clue how I was really feeling. He didn't have a clue I had just drunk texted the guy I was still obsessed with. If he did, I doubt he would have slept with me. No, he would have wanted me to talk about it and be the caring person he is.

That next day I cried and cried and cried, again with what felt like one of the worst hangovers I've ever felt, and riddled with anxiety. After this encounter, I started to notice that wherever I was, I wasn't fully present. When I was on my own in my house I wanted to be surrounded by people, but when I was surrounded by people, I was agitated and wanted to be on my own. For weeks on end, I would count down the days until the weekend. I couldn't wait to drop Noah off at Chris' on Saturday afternoon so I could start drinking. I knew that way I could get blind drunk and forget everything. But every Saturday, I'd reach a certain point when my emotions would build up, and I would break down. It could be the smallest trigger – a sad song or an in-depth conversation with someone. I would sob and sob, telling anyone who would listen how I felt because I needed someone to help me; I couldn't help myself at this point. I was still hopeful that someone would click their fingers and make the pain go away.

There were nights when I buried my head in my hands, uncontrollably crying, my friends trying to pull me together, but their words fell on deaf ears because I wasn't ready to hear them. I wouldn't have Noah back until Sunday night, so that was even worse – having the whole day on my own, hungover and full of dread thinking about whatever I did or said the night before. There were some Sundays where I cried in bed for hours on end, thinking about the drunken texts I'd sent to people, the crying, the blurting out all of my secrets. It was slowly killing me.

During those weeks, there wasn't a single day that I didn't cry. I returned to the salon but I felt so unmotivated, like I was stripped of my passion. I didn't love my job anymore. I felt nothing – I was numb to everything. Do you know how disturbing it is to have your three-year-old ask you, "Why are you crying, Mummy? What's wrong?" "Have you fallen over Mummy, is that why you are sad?" The nights that he was at Chris', I would sleep until midday. Not wanting to get up, feeling like I had nothing apart from him to get up for. But when Noah was at home, when he woke around eight o'clock (I know I already have it good), I couldn't even bear to get up out of bed. Every morning I would hand him his iPad for at least an hour, sometimes two, until I could think about facing the world. Noah was taking such a huge hit that I was feeling so low. I couldn't bring myself to make an effort to cook healthy dinners, so we would have McDonald's or frozen food dinners every night. This was not the mum that I ever wanted to be.

Every time I went out in my car I would purposely play sad songs, singing at the top of my lungs as I cried my heart out. Exercising, seeing my friends, the salon, all the things I loved and used to make me feel better didn't even touch the sides. I was getting worse and worse with social media: constantly looking for gratification from comments and likes, posting a picture of myself smiling when I knew I was miserable inside, searching for things that I knew would hurt me, obsessing over other women and how they looked and how happy they seemed. It was social suicide. I had a full-blown breakdown to Lucy because she uploaded a picture to social media in which I thought I looked terrible. I couldn't control the tears and begged her to take it down. I was tearing myself apart. I fucking hated myself.

She's dangerous when she's hurt, she can easily destroy everything around her, but she doesn't. Instead, she destroys herself.

~Unknown

I couldn't stand the thought of being happy for anyone else. It was so ugly. I couldn't shake the feeling that everyone was moving on in their lives, and that I was being left behind. Two of my close friends told me they were pregnant during this time, a few weeks apart, and it felt like a slap in the face. Lucy had just gotten into a relationship and was the happiest she had ever been, but I tried to shut it off when she spoke about it. Amy had just moved into her beautiful brand-new first home, but I was just so jealous. Another good friend, Charlotte, was starting to get back on the dating scene after being single for a year, but I secretly hoped that the dates would be a disaster. I couldn't be happy for anyone because I was so miserable inside. I just wallowed in my own misery, wondering why this was happening to me. Why were none of my other friends suffering right now? Why was it just me? What have I done to deserve feeling like this?

I needed to get away so I went to Liverpool for a couple of days to see my brother and his fiancé, who I hadn't seen in nearly five months. But again, I started drinking the second I got there at noon. After thirteen hours of drinking, I was sobbing into the firepit, telling my brother how I would die alone and that no one would ever want or love me. At one o'clock in the morning, instead of jumping into bed like any normal drunk person, I went on to have phone sex with a guy that I barely knew.

She's not getting drunk for the hell of it. She's getting drunk to numb the hell of it.

~Sean Bates

I was just existing. I couldn't remember what happiness felt like. I physically didn't know how to get out of this slump. I started to think, *do I need to go to the doctors? Should I ask to go on antidepressants? Is this temporary, or is there seriously something wrong with me?* Convincing myself there was a chemical imbalance in my head, I spent my days Googling wellness retreats and getaways, but then I would talk myself out of booking anything. It just felt like I was masking my problems – a temporary fix. I knew I'd feel amazing if I went, but then I would have to come back to reality, and things wouldn't be any different. Been there, done that, got the t-shirt. I thought at this point that nothing could make me feel better. I was well and truly lost: far, far worse than New Year's Eve.

Somehow it still got worse.

Everything that I had been through, all these men I had been with, shattered my soul. One by one, they had taken parts from me, and it had left me empty. I was torn apart inside. All these men had left their mark on me. I was scarred by each and every one of them. I had no self-esteem, no self-worth, no self-respect, no confidence, and I hated every single part of myself.

I wanted all the pain to go away, so off I went to another party and drank non-stop until five o'clock in the morning.

I was so fucked that my friends were worried that I'd end up in hospital having my stomach pumped. I had never consumed so much alcohol in my life, only to hurl it all back up later. The next morning, after two hours of sleep, it hit me. *What if something had happened to me last night? What if I did end up in the hospital and I was seen as an unfit mother or something worse?* Noah would grow up without a mother and would have to learn it was because of alcohol. What the fuck was I doing to myself? It was the wake-up call I needed.

I knew the first thing to do was stop drinking and having sex; two things that I loved dearly but were becoming extremely toxic for me. So, I went cold turkey.

***

As I approached five weeks without a drop of alcohol or sex, I thought I was on the road to recovery. I hadn't drunk texted anyone. I hadn't spoken to any males, in fact. I was so desperate to feel OK. I thought *I can do this, I can be on my own, no problem.* I thought fixing external things would cure me when really it was the internal things that were still eating away at me, and with a simple phone call, I slipped straight back to the Elle that I had been five weeks earlier.

"Have you seen Shane's in Marbella in a villa with loads of women?" said Amy. You know that sunken-heart feeling you get? Yeah, I got that. From that second, I tortured myself by watching his Instagram stories and all the stories of the women he was with. *Psycho alert!* I couldn't help myself. Then in broad daylight, clear as a day, I came across a picture of him and a woman all cosied up, her arms wrapped around his waist. Why do we do these things when we know it is only going to make us feel like utter shit?

I needed a quick fix. I didn't want to feel wanted. I *needed* to feel wanted. So that evening, I arranged to meet a guy that I knew in a hotel and fucked him. Well, actually, he fucked me. For the first time in my life, I felt frigid. I lay there with this guy on top of me, feeling like every inch of my confidence had been sucked out of me. I went right back to begging for the lights off and even leaving my top and bra on. My nipples didn't get hard. I couldn't even get wet. I thought to myself, *this is it. My body is literally giving up on me. Even my body is telling me not to have sex.* I felt completely paralysed. It didn't make me feel anything. I felt broken inside. Like I no longer had a soul, just a body lying there, with a penis inside me. Within an hour of stepping foot in the hotel, I was back in my car, stone-cold sober and feeling like a fucking prostitute.

The following day it was like clockwork. I got a message from Amy. "Shane told me to tell you he says hello." What? Why would he say that? He's living his best life, surrounded by women on holiday, getting all the attention he so desperately wants. I broke my drinking ban and messaged him, "Why would you tell Amy that? Can you not just say it yourself?"

A blunt "OK" was all I received back. Amy called me later telling me that he had Facetimed her, drunk, rambling on about how he can't talk to me because I'm "too intense". I sent him another message, this time asking him to leave me alone. I told him he was bang out of order for shutting me down again through my best friend. The following day I received a set of messages.

Elle… I'm pretty fucked. I'm so sorry.

What exactly is it you're sorry for?

I can't read that message right now and give you the reply you deserve.

I didn't understand what he wanted from me. Was he apologising for reaching out, or was he apologising for hurting my feelings, yet again?

Elle, please can we talk tomorrow?

I replied that I wouldn't hold my breath.

A whole two days went by without a sound from him. Why the fuck was I waiting around for this guy? I had already been through this. OK, he was on holiday, but for fuck sake, don't put a time on things if you're not going to stick to it. In reality, there was nothing he could possibly say to make me feel better, so what on earth was I holding on for?

By the third day, I received three words from him: *I'm still drunk*. I couldn't believe that he had been that blind drunk for three days straight that he couldn't function to write a message, especially when he was functioning well enough to upload Instagram stories and comment on other women's pictures. Yes, of course, I knew his every move.

I'm not sure what you want to say to me. You clearly don't give a shit about my feelings.

He quickly responded: *I do care about you Elle, I just don't want to be in a relationship right now.*

There they were, the five words that meant so much to me; *I do care about you.* I told him it was never about being in a relationship. It was about how he changed his mind about me quickly. How he went from hot to cold so fast.

He replied, "Because going away changed my opinion, " and a whole new can of worms spilt open in my head. *Why? Why? Why?* I had so many questions but decided to go with another one of my famous essays, telling him how much it hurt to hear that someone could change their mind that quickly, and for fucking over a woman with a soft heart. That was the gist of it. *Obviously.*

Then came another two days of silence. My mind was in overdrive. I was torturing myself. Every hour I was checking strangers' accounts on my Instagram. One thing about me – I will never bother with making a fake account. Fuck that. I have absolutely no shame in stalking people and watching their stories on my own account. I barely slept for those two nights. I was just so angry. How could he leave me hanging like that?

After another three days, I knew I couldn't allow him to consume my moods anymore. I wasn't stupid. I knew deep down Shane didn't give a fuck about me, but I still held out hope that he really did mean what he said. So I sent him one final horrible message and blocked him. I regret this, as I'm not a nasty person, but I couldn't hold my anger in.

And she was made to appear crazy by the man who drove her there.

~R.H. Sin

It's spine-chilling how someone I met just once could have this much of an effect on me. I have such an addictive personality it scares me. It had been six months since we first began talking, and I was ready to be over it. I will never ever get the answers I want. Shane can tell me he didn't want a relationship (which I never said I wanted). He is entitled to change his opinion, which everyone is, as shit as it is. But to tarnish my personality, to say I'm too deep and I'm too intense is where it hurts. That is the person I am. He painted me as being too much for having feelings for someone, and that is where it breaks me down. He put the blame on me. How am I supposed to whittle down my personality? To not be too much? Not be as intense? Not be as deep? To not have feelings?

The answer? I am not. I should never ever change myself for anyone else, and it was time to fucking realise this.

You cannot make everyone think and feel as deeply as you do. This is your tragedy, because you understand them but they do not understand you.

~Daniel Saint

I knew I couldn't get over Shane because I didn't have anyone else to take my mind off it. The difference was, this time, I didn't want to. It was time to stop. Almost a year of being single was on the horizon, and it was time to stop distracting myself with everything I had been through. All I wanted to do was book a one-way flight out of here, but I couldn't because of Noah. And let's be honest, escaping won't change you if you don't deal with what's going on in your head and your heart. I was ready to pull the band-aid off. I knew it was going to sting, I knew I would go through the most uncomfortable healing process, but it was time to heal.

I sat with grief, and I embraced it. I didn't go out and get drunk as a skunk or go out and shag some guy that didn't deserve me. I sat and allowed myself to be sad.

Chapter Twelve
Therapy

Nothing takes more courage than putting yourself back together again.

~The Better Man Project

They say the healing can be worse than the hurt. My God, don't I know it. My life took a 360-degree turn, and for a long time I didn't know how to deal with it. My emotions had spiralled out of control and everything felt so distant, so untouchable, so uncontrollable, so unattainable. Whether I felt sad or angry, I felt it a hundred times over. I was really starting to wonder whether I was emotionally stable. I knew I wanted to heal, but I didn't know how to. I didn't know where to start.

After endless chats with my girlfriends and the advice they gave me, I took the enormous step of contacting a therapist and starting cognitive behavioural therapy (CBT). My first ever session was like when the water started to sink the *Titanic.* The floodgates just wouldn't close. It was hard to open up to a stranger, but once I did, I even felt attached to her. I knew within just ten minutes of talking that it was one of the best decisions of my life. It had been a long time coming. "You're not broken, you're just damaged. You are fixable, I promise, " is what my therapist said in that first session as I sat there uncontrollably crying, struggling to catch my breath, begging her, "Please, please fix me."

My therapist explained that I was going through grief and that I needed to stop distracting myself from the loss I was experiencing. Somebody doesn't have to die for you to experience grief and loss. If you look into the cycle of grief, it is from loss, from situations such as illness, death or a major change in life circumstances. When a person suffers a major loss, they will go through certain grieving stages to heal. Since Kilimanjaro, I had experienced the biggest change in my life by splitting with Chris and cancelling our wedding. I went through a series of emotional states again and again, like a merry go round until I could start the process of recovery.

The first stage I went through was denial. I was numb to the situation and avoided the pain by finding men to have sex with. I pushed the end of the relationship to the back of my mind. The second stage I went through was guilt. I felt responsible for all the pain I had caused Chris and the people around me; I was constantly confused about life and uncertain about my future and what path it was going to take. The third stage was about bargaining. I was begging for God, for anyone who would listen to just take away the pain. The fourth and final stage was sadness, although I'd even go as far as saying I was depressed. I was overwhelmed by every single emotion. I was at rock bottom, and I didn't know how to claw myself back up from the dirt.

Grief isn't a competition, but it's almost easier to grieve someone who you will never see again. You don't have to go through the constant thoughts of whether it was the right decision or not. But when you lose someone who is still alive, you have to live your life knowing that person is still there. And just because I was the one in control of losing someone doesn't make it any easier.

One of the hardest things you'll ever have to do, my dear, is grieving the loss of a person who is still alive.

~Jeannette Walls

I am neither ashamed nor embarrassed for seeking therapy. I wish it was as normalised as it is in the US because it's incredible, and I know many people who would benefit from it (cough cough, a few men I have had encounters with). No one forced me to go – a therapist didn't show up on my doorstep like a fairy godmother. I had to take that step and actually want to be fixed.

Thanks to therapy, I finally understood why I had gotten so low. I can now hold my hands up and admit that I did not actually deal with the end of my ten-year relationship, someone I had spent more than a third of my life with –someone who I thought I was going to spend the rest of my life with, someone I had a child with. I didn't mourn the relationship when I should have. For a year, I masked it and added to the heartache with other men. And when it all came crashing down, it was a pain I had never felt before. It was like a cake, layer upon layer upon layer, none of which I had digested.

The next step was mourning. I mourned, and I mourned. It had been a year of being single, and my God, how I cried. I hadn't cried about Chris for months. I hadn't really talked about him in months. In fact, I was too busy crying over Shane, or the last stupid thing I did. I needed to grieve. I wasn't just grieving a person; I was grieving a life that I thought I would have. I was grieving the loss of the big house we were going to move into, the perfect wedding day we were going to have with all our friends, the second baby we were going to try for this year.

The day we were supposed to get married arrived. I know to some people it's just a date, but to me it was so much more than that. The second my eyes opened that morning, the river came rushing down. And it didn't stop all day. Imagining what it would have been like, imagining walking down the aisle, imagining his face when he saw me, imagining Noah being surrounded by all his favourite people, with mummy and daddy all dressed up and him in his little matching suit.

I took my therapist's advice: I sat with grief, and I embraced it. I didn't go out and get drunk as a skunk. I didn't go out and shag some guy that didn't deserve me. I sat and allowed myself to be sad.

The next day, it was like a huge weight had been lifted off my shoulders. I finally felt at peace, like that was the last thing I needed to mourn from the relationship. It was the last piece of the puzzle to complete. I no longer had the black cloud of guilt hanging over me. I had carried it for far too long. I was worried about how his life was going to be now, worried that he wouldn't ever be happy again. But as harsh as it sounds, that isn't my problem. I can care about him, I always will do, but I can't carry the weight of someone else's feelings on my shoulders. I finally forgave not only what he did but myself. I forgave myself for tearing someone's life apart and breaking up a family.

"No-one will ever make you happy. You will always want more." That was one of the last things Chris said to me when we broke up. And I think he was right. I realise it was me that was deeply unhappy, and you will never be happy with someone else if you aren't happy with yourself, and that's a fact.

Maybe, true happiness is when we are happy with ourselves.

~Faraway

When I was at my lowest, I had booked to go to Ibiza with Amy. I needed a break. I had only been in therapy a month when the date came to leave. I was starting to feel really good on the inside, but I won't lie and pretend I wasn't riddled with anxiety that a foot-loose and fancy-free holiday could trigger me to go back to my old ways. *What if I drink too much? Will I come back wanting to drink more? What if I have sex with someone and regret it? What if I go to sleep with someone and I am still a corpse just lying there?* Everything was swarming around my mind, but the second I got there I knew it was going to be one of the best holidays I had ever had. Seriously, I was young, free and happy. Also supporting brand-new long dark locks (new hair, new me bullshit again). For the first time in my life, I felt happy to be single. No drama to deal with back home, no one to answer to, no worries in the morning wondering what on Earth I did the night before. Let's just say that I enjoyed myself to the fullest. I felt more powerful than ever before that I could have a one-night stand and enjoy it for exactly what it is, not for any other reason – I definitely got my mojo back!

To be able to be happy again, I had to let the pain go. You have got to mourn what happened to you and what you feel, regardless of whether it's the love of your life breaking up with you or the guy you really like ghosting you. We need to make it more known that it is okay not to be okay. It's okay to be sad, to be heartbroken over a relationship that ended, to have your heart shattered by a guy you never dated, to feel upset about being second best or not good enough, to feel like you want to give up. *It's okay.* But you must feel it. Let it all out. Because there is nothing worse than pretending not to care or pretending not to feel anything.

The bravest thing you can do is be unafraid to feel.

~Bridgett Devoue

I had never been so ashamed of myself. Ever.

Chapter Thirteen
The Relapse

Be careful fighting someone else's demons – it may awaken your own.

~Bryant McGill

Save the best until last, right? I told the world that I was about to share my story, but how naïve to think it was finished. Jason told me everything I wanted to hear and, unfortunately, everything I needed to hear. The one man who I thought treated me exactly how I deserved to be treated turned out to be the worst of them all.

Everything was perfect (famous last words). Things at the salon were starting to look up again as I had finally hired two new stylists, and I wasn't looking for any man to entertain. But as the saying goes, it always happens when you're not looking for it. They say it happens when you're breezing through life happy as ever, minding your own business – that's when someone will come along. That's what I thought this was. I thought I'd found what I'd been waiting for. I thought I'd stumbled upon my "big meant to be" moment at last.

I wasn't supposed to be at the pub that evening. Lucy and I had a party to go to, but she was there with her girlfriend and their friends, and I was supposed to just pull up outside and pick her up. I felt overdressed, but after much persuasion I agreed to join them for one drink. Walking into an unknown place full of people I don't know always sends my social anxiety sky high. I remember trying to focus on the door in front of me, but before I knew it my vision was blurred, and then suddenly it became fixated on someone I had never seen before. *Who the hell is that?*

Jason turned out to be very good friends with everyone I was meeting, but I had never heard of him before. From the offset, the eye contact was on. Every time I looked at him, he was already looking at me. I would shy away and take a sip of my drink, but I couldn't resist – my eyes were drawn back to him over and over again. As the evening drew in and conversation flowed, Jason came to sit next to me. He had these unusual caramel-coloured eyes that looked like freshly stirred coffee with cream. Jesus, those eyes. He had me in stitches of laughter from the second he sat down, and our conversation was non-stop. He had a son, so we shared stories about our children and experiences of parenthood. It didn't take long for things to get a little deeper, talking about how and why we were both single. He even opened up about his best friend, who had tragically lost his life six months prior, and the pain it had caused. It seemed like we had a lot in common, and I couldn't help but be drawn to him. He was so open. We even chatted about previous relationships and why they hadn't worked out – both agreeing that genuine affection is a must-have. With that, he politely asked if he could place his hand on my leg, which of course I obliged to, with my hand being all over his seconds later.

He struck me as being in touch with his feelings, someone with a hard exterior but soft on the inside. I saw that side to him immediately. Earlier I'd overheard a conversation about him having somewhat of a violent past which surprised me.

"I hope what you heard earlier doesn't change your opinion of me, " he said. I told him it didn't, and I was honest. Everyone has a past, and I will never judge anyone based on their history. People change and better themselves all the time – if anything, it makes them more intriguing. There was so much more to him than met the eye.

There was something in your eyes. Your eyes spoke to me a million things.

~Avijeet Das

After staying two hours too long, we had to leave for the party. Jason followed me on Instagram and said, "I'm not going to message you first. I've made the first move." Stubborn from the get-go, but I liked it. I got in the car grinning from ear to ear, telling Lucy how I never thought I would fancy anyone ever again, and yet here I was, fancying the pants off someone I'd met by chance.

I played it cool and waited until the next day to message him. It wasn't long until he replied, telling me how nice it had been to meet me. Within a matter of hours, he asked me for my number. He said he wanted to tell me something over the phone. I shuddered at the thought of what he was about to say and convinced myself he probably had a girlfriend. To my surprise, he called to ask me out on a date. "I know you might think this is super keen, but I really want to take you out. Are you free tomorrow night?" *Jesus, tomorrow night?* That *is* keen. He went on to say he was having an operation to fix his broken nose the following day, so he wouldn't be able to see me for a while after. I couldn't help but blush. This guy really wanted to see me and wasn't willing to wait a couple of weeks. My heart was pounding. *A date, an actual date, with an actual man.* It was something I hadn't done for more than six years. I swallowed all my negative thoughts and said yes.

The next evening arrived, and I was a bag of nerves. Lucy came over to calm me down as I got ready, trying on every outfit under the sun. Hundreds of thoughts were spinning around my head. *What if he doesn't like me? What if I don't like him? What if we have nothing to talk about? What if my word vomit comes up?*

He booked a steakhouse restaurant and told me to be ready for seven o'clock. I guzzled a glass of wine for courage while pacing my entire house, questioning whether or not I could actually go through with it. Too late, he was here. I got in his car, kissed him on the cheek, and we both complimented each other. Within minutes I felt calm.

There wasn't a single second of awkward silence between us. We rarely came up for air from talking as the conversation just kept spilling out of us. He wouldn't leave my hands or legs alone, and I couldn't leave his alone either. I told him how nervous I had been earlier, and he confessed that he had been just as nervous and had nearly turned his car around on the way to pick me up. Even though my nerves had subsided, my clumsy side still managed to make an appearance, as I knocked the table and our drinks went flying. I made light that I'm a klutz and told Jason how I struggle with eye contact because of my anxiety. But somehow, his eye contact settled me, even though it was intense. The way he looked at me, it was as if his eyes never left me.

He looked at her the way all women want to be looked at by a man.

~F. Scott Fitzgerald

"What are you celebrating?" The waitress smiled. As we sniggered away, she continued to ask questions. "How long have you been together, are you married?" I placed my head in my hands, unable to control the laughter as Jason explained that we had only just met. "Two days ago, actually, " he added. Her face was a picture, in complete and utter shock. She didn't believe us and thought we were lying to her. Not only was I having an amazing time, but it also appeared that the whole restaurant could see it too. Like the true gentleman he seemed to be, he paid for the meal but not before the waitress had one last say. "You two are amazing together. I think you will stay together." *Wow, could this date get any better?*

Apparently, it could. We walked out to the car park hand in hand, and just as we reached his car he pulled me in and kissed me. My God, I swear I could see the sparks flying. He opened his car door for me, but then we just sat there kissing for a while, fixated on each other. "I would say let's go for a coffee but everywhere will be shut now, " he said.

"You can come to mine for a coffee if you want, " I replied. *No no no!* For the first time in probably forever, I didn't want it to be like that, I wanted it to be *just* a date, but I couldn't help myself. I didn't want the night to end.

I didn't even get a chance to boil the kettle. We immediately started kissing like teenagers on the sofa. His hands didn't move from my face, though. He gave no indication of wanting anything more than to just kiss me. He started laughing and tried to utter some words but would backtrack as soon as he started. Eventually, he blurted it out. "I can't believe I'm saying this, but that's the best date I have ever been on!" My face warmed as my grin spread from ear to ear. I didn't have many dates to compare to, so it was easy for me to carry on blushing and agree.

He had so much passion, kissing me in between his sentences, touching my neck and my face so softly while I lingered on his every word. I was four large wines deep and couldn't deny how attracted I was to him, so I took it to the next level. I straddled him, but he quickly picked me up under my thighs and swung me around so I was on my back before grinding his body against mine. It was as if he wanted control. I tried to take it back, grabbing his hand and leading him upstairs.

Lying on my bed, I could have kissed him for hours. He unbuttoned his shirt slowly as I tried to take in how beautiful he was. He slowly slipped me out of my jeans and worked his way back up, kissing every inch of my legs. The higher and higher he got, the shorter my breath became. He paused at the inside of my thighs for a few seconds before reaching for my black lace knickers and sliding them down. *Oh, the build-up.* My legs started to shake instantly as he let his tongue circle slowly and his fingers enter me. It was the perfect dose of hard and slow.

We writhed around, pressing our hot naked bodies together – his fingers pleasuring me. "I don't want to sleep with you, " he said, brushing the hair away from my face. Hearing the words as they left his mouth, he quickly corrected himself. "Of course, I want to sleep with you, but I like you, and I don't want you to think that's all I'm here for or that that's the reason I asked you out."

Wow. No man has ever respected me that much. I didn't feel rejected. I felt like this man liked me for me. Just me. As I lay down beside him, feeling giddy with butterflies in my stomach, I found myself lost in thought. *I'm not broken. I can feel again.*

We made our way back downstairs to have a late-night coffee together. As he got up to leave, he turned to me. "I really like you. Can I take you on a second date?" My stomach did somersaults, and, of course, I said yes. Grinning like a Cheshire cat as I closed the door behind him, I let out an almighty sigh of relief.

The next day, as soon as I opened my eyes, I turned to my phone to see if he'd messaged. He had! It read: *Good morning, beautiful*, with lots of love hearts. This soon became his thing, sending me that same message every morning and *Goodnight* every evening.

It was the day of his operation, so I didn't think he would have much time to be chatting with me. I put no pressure on him, but he rang me pretty much the second he got home. He'd been telling his friends and family about me and how well our date went. Apparently, his mum said how much of an amazing couple we would be and how well suited we seemed. We joked about how everyone had already married us off – even the waitress! He was in a world of pain and started to show me pictures from his surgery. The conversation turned to cosmetic surgery, and I admitted there were certain procedures I had considered. "You are beautiful as you are, " he gushed. "Not just to look at – you are a beautiful person inside, too." The guy had me blushing from the second I woke to the moment I went to sleep.

That evening, after I put Noah to bed, he politely asked if he could call me again. Two hours later, we finally got off the phone. This quickly became our routine, and every night I would look forward to his call. I had completely forgotten what it felt like to go to bed with a smile on my face because of someone else. It had been such a long time. The thing I loved most about our conversations was how deep things got. I didn't feel awkward. It felt natural to talk to him about anything and everything. He told me a lot about his past, and I did the same. I found him so understanding, and it wasn't long before he told me that I could trust him.

I did trust him. It sounds crazy because we barely knew each other, but we were already sharing secrets and had both been so open from the moment we met; it just felt right. He admitted he found it hard to show his soft side with some people, but with me, he had no qualms. I confided in him about my fears with the impending book release, and he reassured me that I had nothing to worry about, that it was an amazing achievement – something to be proud of. He had such a way with words that when they poured out of him, it felt as though they were literally seeping into my skin. I absorbed everything he had to say, and he made me feel safe.

As the days passed by, his recovery seemed to be going a lot better than he initially thought it would, so he asked if he could see me again soon. He said he couldn't wait much longer, and all that he wanted was to kiss and hug me. The closer it got, the more intense our relationship became. He asked if we would have our first photo when I saw him and told me his son would love Noah. He told me he hadn't stopped talking about me, telling all his friends and family how infatuated he was. Out of nowhere, a fear pierced through my body like an electric shock. *No, this is too much. I was so happy single, now he's taking up all my time. My time that I had fought so desperately hard to have so that I could be happy on my own.*

That Friday, I saw my therapist. I told her every single thing about him, every minute detail and every last word we'd exchanged. At first, I felt like I was almost gloating about how incredible I thought he was, but as I said the words out loud, I felt nauseous, panicking; it was too much too soon. "Maybe I'd feel more comfortable if he backed off. If he didn't reply one day. I do like to be kept on my toes after all."

My therapist warned me I was at risk of slipping back into my old toxic traits. But it was hard not to. That was what I had become accustomed to – men coming and going from my life as they pleased. *Fucking hell Elle, this is all you've ever wanted, a guy who is straight up telling you he is not speaking to anyone else, telling you he isn't interested in anyone else, that he is fully invested in you. A man that is finally telling you not only how beautiful you are on the outside but how beautiful you are as a person, and you're thinking of walking away because it's too much too soon?* Erratic maybe, but I knew the higher the intensity of something, the further the fall.

If someone makes you feel, let them.

~Reyna Biddy

Two nights before our second date, things got deeper still. He was drinking with friends and texted me: *I do really, really like you, Elle. I can't wait to get to know you even more, even though I already feel like I know you so well.* A few drinks later: *I was so nervous and bothered about what you thought of me, but I literally can't wait to date you more and more. I find myself talking about you to everyone. I had given up. I didn't think I would ever have a connection with anyone, but then I met you for an hour, and we clicked.*

I was so overwhelmed with everything he was saying. I thought: *How can this person be real right now?* Surely this is too good to be true? I tried to keep my feet firmly on the ground and texted him back: *We have just got to take each day as it comes, but I can't wait to see you again too.*

He replied: *I know, I know, take it slow. But I really hope it happens. All my mates know I'm smitten with you. I love your smile. The best thing is I know you've got a kind heart, and that's all I want.*

It was finally time for date number two. I drove to his house and we took a stroll to the Chinese restaurant down the road, holding hands and kissing each other like we were an official couple. The second date was just as good as the first, if not better. In between the continuous laughter and sexual attraction, the conversation was meaningful. He seemed to really care about my wellbeing as I opened up about my battles with anxiety. I described how hard it was with someone that didn't understand anxiety or just brushed it under the carpet whenever I spoke about it or felt like it was creeping up. His eyes glossed over, and a tear hit his cheek. He quickly put his hand over his face and apologised for getting upset. I asked him to tell me what was wrong, was it something I said?

Opening up, he explained how he had suffered from anxiety when he lost his best friend, although, at the time, he didn't understand what he was going through and that he didn't want anyone to ever feel like that again. I grabbed his hand, squeezed it and really took in this person that was in front of me, someone who was still in a lot of pain. He quickly moved away from the subject. He said he couldn't talk about it, or he would break down. I kissed his hand. "It's OK, we don't have to talk about it, or we can whenever you want to."

Midway through our meal, as if he couldn't hold it in any longer, he asked me if I would go away with him somewhere. "A log cabin, a hotel, anywhere?"

I knew things were moving incredibly fast, but I couldn't help it. I was well and truly swept up in our connection. "Of course, I would love to!"

As we left the restaurant and started to walk back to his, I had a cigarette. He had mentioned during one of our many phone calls how much he disliked smoking after quitting his thirty-a-day habit many years ago, but he didn't seem to mind as I lit up. This time we went straight into his kitchen and put the kettle on. After a couple of sips of tea, we were already locking lips. This time it was more passionate. He pinned me against his kitchen unit and covered me in kisses all around my neck. His hands moved from my face down my body, grasping every part of me. I tried to be as gentle as I could with him, bearing in mind he was still recovering from his operation, but I wanted to return the intensity, return the passion. As we stumbled across his kitchen, not saying a word, he started to kiss me slowly and ran his fingers over the scar on my chest. I flinched and began to explain what the scar was from. Before I could finish my sentence, he said, "I know what that scar is from. You don't have to say anything, " and kissed me so gently. At that very moment, I was smitten too. I wanted him; I wanted every part of him.

Jason took the plunge this time, grabbing my hand and leading me up the stairs. We barely touched the bed as he undressed me. I tried to undress him too, but again, with his recovery, it was hard to do it in any sexy shape or form. At this point I knew I liked him, not because we were about to have sex, but because of how nervous I was. I hadn't had sex with someone that I liked in so long. The way he touched me, the way he didn't take his eyes off me… The second he went down on me, my legs started to shudder. The very thought of him made my whole body tremble. I pulled him up, whispering, "I want you to fuck me." He gently pushed me back and eased himself inside of me. I was right. He definitely liked to be in control. He was more of a giver than a taker. As he got deeper and deeper, I had the urge to grab the back of his neck, pull him in closer to me, but I could see the discomfort in his eyes. I kept apologising, asking if he wanted to stop, but he persisted, trying his very best to not look like he wasn't in excruciating pain. He spread my legs open wide to go down on me again, but I could see he was hurting from his operation, so we stopped.

I wasn't bothered that it wasn't out-of-this-world sex, I wasn't bothered that it didn't last long, I wasn't bothered that it wasn't wild and rough how I would normally like it. For the first time, I started to look into the future. I lay there and thought, well, we are definitely going to have a lot more opportunities at this, and to my surprise, he took the words right out of my mouth. "It's only going to get better from here." We both laughed, cuddled up to each other.

The following day his work got called off, so it meant he had a free afternoon. It was only ten o'clock when he told me to get the kettle on as he was coming round. *Shit, in the day?* The last three times he'd seen me I had always been dolled up, with a full face of makeup, false eyelashes and perfectly curled hair, but I didn't have time to do any of that! I was petrified that he would walk through the door and think I was a completely different person to who he took out on a date last night, but I knew I couldn't keep up the pretence that I look that polished twenty-four/seven because, well, I don't.

I needn't have worried. The minute he stepped into my home, he told me I looked beautiful. He brought his new puppy around, and just like that, the three of us were cuddled up on the sofa. It was so relaxed, as if we had known each other for months – years even – so relaxed that he began to rest his head on my shoulders and fell asleep for twenty minutes. There was kissing, of course there was kissing, but there was no sign of anything else. I couldn't believe someone wanted to just be with me, even if it was just for two hours – to just be with me and not have sex.

How beautiful it is to find someone who asks for nothing but your company.

~Brigitte Nicole

That evening we had another lengthy phone call, as if we really couldn't get enough of each other. It was getting late, and I yawned and told him I was crying.

"Why are you crying?!"

"Because I yawned, silly. I'm not actually crying."

"Oh good, I never ever want to make you cry." This man exceeded all my expectations of how a woman should really be treated – how *I* deserved to be treated. "If I'm honest, I don't even feel single right now."

There was a silence for a few seconds. He might even have heard me gasp for air. The sudden panic came rushing back. What does he mean? If he doesn't feel single, what does that make us? Do I want to be in a relationship? Is this going far too quickly? I wanted to take things slow. My head was spinning, and all I could muster was, "Well, you know I am not speaking to anyone else either."

Just two days later, he was eager to see me again. We spoke on the phone on and off all day, and he dropped plenty of hints, telling me he had no plans the following Friday evening, that no one was available. I toyed with the idea of having him over, but I was still worried that things had snowballed too fast. Eventually, I decided to go with my heart over my head.

We ordered a pizza and put on a film. I missed this feeling so much, the feeling you get when you're so comfortable around someone that you can literally just eat, talk, laugh and cuddle all night. It really felt like this was going somewhere, that this could be the start of something special. I placed him in between my legs, resting his back against my chest as I massaged his shoulders and arms and kissed his neck.

After a while, he really started to open up about the loss of his best friend. He struggled to talk about it, so I took a big gulp and told him: "You are talking to me as if I know what happened, but I don't. You don't have to tell me if you don't want to, but you can tell me anything, you know that."

I felt the tension ease away from his shoulders as tears came streaming down his face. He told me the horrific events around the death. I held his hand the entire time, stroking his arm, just listening. If I could have taken his pain away there and then, I would have. He explained that when he told his ex-girlfriend the tragic news, she stood there and put her hands on her hips and told him she didn't know what to say. *You know what? I didn't know what to say either*. I felt hopeless. I wasn't with him when it happened and I didn't know the person that passed away. All I could do was be there for him as he so bravely opened up to me. When he finished, I slowly placed myself on his lap and just hugged him as I could feel his tears on my chest. "You're literally amazing, " he whispered.

I want to hold hands and waste Friday nights with you.

~Unknown

The weekend arrived, and he had a busy couple of days planned with his son while I was working and doing a photoshoot. We knew we would struggle to see each other, so we instead decided to make plans for the following weekend. He wanted to take me to see his favourite West-End show in London and stay the night there, and I suggested we plan a double date with our mutual friends. It was exciting to be planning ahead with someone I had feelings for.

As I wrapped up my photoshoot, I rang him on my way home. "Do you want to come round for a cup of tea?" he asked. My body froze. I knew what he was really asking was if I wanted to meet his son. Things were moving at lightning speed, but as I took a step back, I reminded myself that it was his decision, not mine. And while I was nowhere near ready for him to meet Noah, he clearly felt comfortable with me meeting his son.

I threw on some tracksuit bottoms and a baggy open shirt to try and tone down the full makeup and hair I still had on from my shoot. I was a nervous wreck driving to his house, going over every possible scenario in my head. *What if his son doesn't want to talk to me? What if I don't know what to say to him? What if he hates me?* It was as if I thought I was incapable of holding a conversation with a child. But I knew they had a very close, untouchable relationship, so that, coupled with the fact that kids don't tend to hold back, filled me with dread in case his son didn't like me.

Jason's son was the sweetest boy and seemed to warm to me, even though I'm sure he could tell how nervous I was. The three of us sat all snuggled up on the sofa, talking about all sorts of things. Jason said he could tell how nervous his son was, but that actually put me at ease. I never thought about being with someone that had a child because I had been so terrified about being with someone who didn't, about them not understanding what life was like when you have a child. But we did have that understanding. We both knew we would never be each other's number one, that we both had other priorities that would always come first. I couldn't stop my mind from running wild, thinking how amazing it would be – the four of us, together, and what little adventures we could have, the places we could go and visit.

Every time his son left the room to get a drink, go to the toilet or when he got ready for bed, Jason would turn to me, kiss me so intensely and rub between my legs. It was so exciting and left me flustered, but the second his son came back in the room, we would giggle and carry on being respectable adults. As I said goodbye to his son, Jason walked me to the front door. He pinned me up tightly against the door, grabbed my face and said, "You look unbelievable, " before planting his lips on mine. I was quite literally weak at the knees. To be a family man one minute, then to be pinning me up against his door the next, everything was just so fitting. I was quick to text him the second I left.

He didn't hate me, did he?

Why the fuck would he? You're so nice, he said how nice you were and that you're really pretty.

My heart felt so full.

You steady me and stir me all at once.

~Butterflies Rising

The following night we had planned to go out to another restaurant together. Jason had work, and I was busy travelling down south for a business meeting that I was incredibly anxious about. He spent most of the day trying to calm me down and ease my worries, and to a certain extent, he did. He made me feel so much better, but that's the thing with anxiety. It never really goes away, even if it appears so on the surface. I was rushing to get ready before he arrived at mine, but twenty minutes before he was due to arrive, he rang to say he would be early as he needed to charge his phone. He told me to unlock my door so he could let himself in while I carried on getting ready so I didn't have to rush. As he pulled up, he took a photo of me getting ready in my dressing room and sent it to me saying how beautiful I looked, but I couldn't help but feel rushed and agitated. Every girl knows the pain of trying to stick her eyelashes on when you are in a hurry. There was a lot of swearing, that's for sure. I became even more flustered when I realised I'd left chapters of my book out on the side, as I didn't have time to tidy. "Don't read my book, will you?" I shouted.

"Of course I won't, " he replied.

Throughout dinner we talked and talked, holding hands and playing footsie under the table. We discussed future dates, and he told me he couldn't wait for me to meet his mum and that he wanted to go for drinks with my parents soon. He even let slip that he was in the middle of booking somewhere for us to go that weekend. But then, like a flick of a switch, something felt off, and I noticed he was on his phone more than ever before. Before long he told me he couldn't be late because he had to collect his puppy from his mum. *Maybe that's who he's texting*, I told myself while biting my fingers nervously whenever he stopped holding my hand to look at his phone. I was really struggling to look at him for longer than a few seconds at a time and could feel a knot in the pit of my stomach. Something was different. I felt all over the place, and it didn't help that I was two large wines deep.

Towards the end of the meal, I had a horrendous stitch. I don't know what caused it, but I told him we needed to leave soon to have a cigarette to calm me down. As we walked outside, he scooped me up from behind and kissed me before we walked hand-in-hand back to my house. He told me he could only come inside for a few minutes because he really had to go and collect his puppy, so as the door shut behind us, I tried to kiss him, but this time he couldn't kiss me. He tried. He tried to pin me up against the wall and snog me, but he kept pulling back, blaming the smell of smoke and how he needed to shoot off to pick up his dog.

I tried to pull my skinny black strap down so he could see the exotic red lacey bra I'd so carefully picked out, ready for what I thought the way the night was going to go. That wasn't even tempting him, so I went and brushed my teeth, but he said he could still smell it on me, that it was everywhere. His words hit me square in the face, and anxiety rippled through my body at the thought of him not liking something about me. I felt my word vomit burning its way up my throat. "Jesus, I dread to think what it'll be like if we ever have an argument." I couldn't take it back as he quizzed me about what I meant. I managed to mumble something about us both being stubborn and that our arguments would probably be awful.

As he put his coat on to leave, he told me I was too pretty to smoke and that it didn't suit me. He kissed me once more as I sat down, trying to hold my sulk in on the bottom step of my stairs. He told me he would see me Wednesday, followed up with, "Just don't have a cigarette before I come, okay?"

Embarrassment and rejection swarmed through my body, and once again, I couldn't hold my tongue. "Maybe I will, maybe I won't."

"Don't be like that. I'll see you Wednesday, " he rolled his eyes.

"I'm going to fuck myself now because you won't. Bye." I blurted out, slamming the door. Like the hole I was digging couldn't get any deeper.

Straight away, I regretted my choice of words. I messaged to try and lighten the mood: *You don't fancy me, do you?* Half an hour later, he replied, telling me he did fancy me and it was just the cigarette smoke he disliked. I was like a dog with a bone and couldn't drop it. He seemed to keep his cool and sent me a nice message with love hearts aplenty, so I replied: *Thank you again for another really nice evening and sorry for being a bit all over the place and also for the whole smoke thing.* But this time I didn't receive a reply.

As my alarm woke my fragile head up, I shot up to glance straight at my phone, trying to search for his name on my home screen. There was no *good morning beautiful*, just *don't worry about it, I've got to go to work now. I'll message you later.* I could instantly tell something was wrong. My gut feeling was right. Something bad was going to happen. We always spoke all day, every day when he was at work, so why today would he message me afterwards?

An hour later, his name popped up: *Elle, I'm really sorry.* Before I read the rest, I slumped on the bed and could feel the colour in my face draining from within me. *I just don't see this progressing into anything further. It's pissed me off, and I feel like shit because I really like you, but something doesn't feel right. It's nothing you've said or done, thank you for the nice times we have spent together xx.*

My heart fucking sank. I burst into tears, wailing into my pillow that this couldn't be happening. I fucking knew it was coming, but that didn't ease the pain at all.

I saw it coming, but at the same time, I didn't because I didn't believe the world could possibly be that fucking cruel.

~Unknown

The tears wouldn't stop coming. I was a blubbering mess on the phone to Lucy trying to make sense of it all. "I'm so confused; it's obviously something I've done." She was trying to comfort me, telling me something had obviously happened, that nobody says all those things to someone and then wakes up the next day and changes their mind. Noah was with me when I received the text. I tried to settle him downstairs so he didn't see me upset, but he wouldn't leave my side. "Mummy, don't cry. It's all going to be OK."

It felt like an eternity, but I left it twenty minutes before I replied. I tried to stay calm. I tried my hardest not to send a lengthy message pouring out my feelings. I simply said that I knew this would happen and that he knew I was absolutely petrified of liking someone for this reason. I admitted I was confused and that I felt like something must have happened for him to change his mind so quickly.

I sat there, completely unable to get my head around it for three hours, with no reply from him. It was the most confused I have ever been with any man, and before I knew it, I was typing a message from the heart: *How can you go wanting to see someone every other day, speaking to them all day every day, having two-hour phone calls, to not even replying to their message?* It was desperation at its finest.

Finally, a reply: *I know how it seems, and that was never my intention, just something yesterday didn't feel right, and I would rather be honest with you. I meant everything I've said previously, and believe me, I never wanted to feel this way. I made efforts because it felt right. Don't beat yourself up. You did nothing wrong. Don't hold back either because you deserve the best. x*

I wish I could have accepted his reason.

Nothing hurts more than a heart left wondering why.

~F.W.

The next morning, my eyes puffy and barely open, I was getting Noah ready for school, styling his hair in front of the mirror. "Mummy, you look so sad. Please don't be sad." The tears came flooding back. I cried that whole day, too, torturing myself about the reasons, ripping myself apart, still asking myself, what didn't feel right that night? I thought that there *had* to be a real reason. There had to be a reason why it ended so soon when it seemed so right. I was petrified I'd lose myself again at the thought of not being good enough. The first man I dated, and it had ended as quickly as it started.

Within the space of two days, he started following forty new women on Instagram. *Forty*. How can you just be done with a person and be so quick to find another? Done with one date on Monday and more than likely have a new date lined up for Saturday. *Was I just a number to him? Just another girl he dated that meant jack shit? Just another notch on his bedpost?* I thought that if this is what the dating world is – a cold, heartless, throwaway kind of world – then I don't want to be a part of it. Telling all your friends and your parents that you've met this amazing guy, and then when they ask you how it's going, you have to go back on your word and say it didn't work out, it's exhausting. I would have kept him to myself. I wouldn't have told my parents about him or all my friends if he didn't tell me he was doing the same; if he didn't give me hope that this had been something with a future.

I thought I was done with begging someone to stay in my life, but I wasn't begging him to stay in my life. I was begging for a reason. I had a full day of hair appointments on Thursday and couldn't concentrate. I kept feeling the overwhelming feeling that I was just going to burst into tears any time I spoke to someone. Two days later and my mind was *still* spinning. Why can't we live in a world where we are all just brutally honest with each other? If you think you don't like something, then say it. Yes, it might hurt their feelings, but what hurts more? Knowing that one thing they didn't like about you, which you will eventually move on from, or constantly wondering why, tearing yourself apart, thinking it was this or it was that? I needed him to be cruel to be kind to me.

Regarding relationships, I have just one rule: Give me the truth, however cold or cruel or hard it is to hear.

~Beau Taplin

I messaged him again: *Were they all lies? Did you not have to go and collect your puppy? Did you just want to get out of my house? Is there someone else?*

He apologised, telling me he understood why I was confused and that the way he went about it probably wasn't the best. He denied my questions and reiterated his reason that there was just something missing for him, and he couldn't figure it out. It didn't help. I didn't get what I wanted or needed. I text: *Why would you give up on someone so easily if you were honest about how much you liked them? Why would you see someone so much if, deep down, you thought something was missing?* I was hitting my head against a brick wall. All I got was another empty apology and a message to say he wouldn't continue the conversation any further.

I had never heard of Jason before I met him but somehow, as fate goes, the weekend after he called things off I found myself in my local pub with one of his closest friends – someone I'd never seen in there before. I was drunk and I couldn't hold the tears back, telling his friend how confused and hurt I was from what had happened. He was shocked himself and tried reaching out to Jason to give me another chance. "No mate, I'm done." *Done?* It was so blunt and so cold. Nothing like the man I thought I'd gotten to know. I continued to get blind-drunk, ignoring all my own advice from my previous chapter.

The distraction carried on, and I slept with two men and a woman all in the space of two weeks. I laughed it off to my friends. "I'm single. I'm not seeing anyone anymore, so I can do whatever the fuck I want!" In reality, I had fallen back to my old ways and was starting to think I had a problem.

We all have "issues" because we all have a story. And no matter how much work you've done on yourself, we all snap back sometimes. So be easy on you. Growth is a dance. Not a light switch.

~John Kim

Maybe it was that I smoked. Even though he knew that from the first time we met each other, maybe something just clicked, and he decided didn't want to be with a smoker. Maybe it was the book. It would take a strong man to be able to be with me, as all my past stories would be open and public to the whole world. Maybe it was because I said I was dreading the time we have an argument. Maybe it was because I am stubborn.

Maybe it was my anxiety. Even though he said he loved how deep I was, and I loved how emotional he was, maybe he thought that two emotional people can't be together, that maybe it would be a recipe for disaster if you are both in need of each other and can't be there for one another.

Maybe it was his own issues and insecurities. He was so hurt by his ex-girlfriend because he thought she had cheated. Cheating repulsed him. He got angry whenever the topic arose, even in a film. Maybe it was because I told him I cheated on my ex eight years ago. Maybe he couldn't be with someone who had done that in the past. Maybe he was just protecting himself. I know how intimidating I can seem with how I look on my Instagram feed and that I have men sliding in my DMs all the time. I know it's intimidating; I've been told a dozen times. Maybe he couldn't be with someone with my lifestyle.

Maybe you were everything, and he wasn't enough. It's not always you, sweetheart.

~R.H. Sin

Maybe, maybe, maybe. I tried to understand that it could have been any one of these reasons, and perhaps the reason was better left unsaid. He wasn't giving me any answers, and I wasn't getting closure, so I decided I needed to do something to help me put it to bed. The longer it went on, the more I could feel myself losing my grip on my emotions, and that's when I did the most irrational thing I have probably ever done. I told my therapist about what I wanted to do. She told me to wait, to wait until my emotions weren't as high, but even she couldn't save me this time. To try and get over the situation, I wrote and wrote until I had everything down on paper. But I didn't stop there. I clearly didn't think that was enough closure. I felt like he needed to know what he'd done. If he knew how I felt and still didn't give me the answers I deserved, it said more about him than it did me. So I sent what I'd written about him to his house with a first-class stamp. Yep, I really did. *(I think I've watched too many films where sending letters is classed as romantic, not completely psychotic.)* The second I did it, I wanted to take it back. I even thought about coming back when the postman was doing his collections and begging, "Excuse me, Sir, please can I have that letter back? I don't want to post it anymore."

Ironically, it didn't give me closure – it opened a whole new can of worms. *I wonder if he's read it. He's probably just tossed it in the bin. God, I really hope he's just thrown it in the bin.* That was it. I was never going to message or speak to him again. He knew how I felt, and he didn't care. Now *I* was done. Well and truly done. That is, until a week later, when his sister and brother-in-law started following me on Instagram. My mind went straight back into overdrive. I don't have a private account, so if people want to stalk me, they can go right ahead, and I'd be none the wiser. But to follow me? They knew I would see that, and it was as if they wanted some kind of reaction. Naturally, a reaction is what they got.

Why is your family following me on Instagram? I fired.

Do not EVER write about me again, he shot back. *I want nothing to do with you, I have started to write my own version of events, and you will get some home truths soon enough as to why I walked away.*

Probably the worst thing you could say to an insecure person who suffers from anxiety.

What are these home truths, then? Come on, tell me.

You will get your chapter when it's ready.

Save me the suspense, and just tell me now.

He didn't answer me. I was like a ticking timebomb about to lose my shit (if you didn't think I had already lost it). I tried to ring him. Only twice, but it was twice too many.

He texted: *You are a fucking fruit-loop.*

Charming. I replied: *EVERYONE says that about you, Jason, everyone!* It is all I could muster in my defence. *Be a man, and fucking tell me.*

YOU WERE A FUCKING BET ELLE! Nothing more and nothing less than a hundred pound bet with my friends that I couldn't get you to go on a date with me and sleep with me. But you did. You are nothing more than just an easy fucking slag.

My hands are shaking as I type this; it is so painful to relive it. Listening to that was one of the most painful things I have ever experienced. That I was nothing more and nothing less than an object, a game to someone. I couldn't believe someone, someone that seemed so understanding, could be that volatile. A man that I had so desperately wanted, telling me everything I wanted to hear, had turned into a cold-hearted monster.

He blocked me before I could lower myself to his level. Remember when I said I would rather someone be as hurtful as they can towards me so I can hate them and move on? Well, I take it back. I learnt the hard way that some things are better left unsaid. I'm not going to lie. It almost broke me reading his spiteful words. Actually, as a matter of fact, it did break me. But this time, for the better.

You made me hate myself a lot.

~Unknown

That night I lay in the bath for two hours until the water turned cold, my eyes stinging and dry from sobbing, hating every single inch of myself. I felt like scrubbing every single layer of my skin off until it was raw. I felt like I was nothing more and nothing less than the words he burned me with. I had never been so ashamed of myself. Ever.

The next morning, I received an apology: *I am sorry things got nasty last night, things between us just went too far, and I never wanted you to find out. I never wanted to argue with you as I'm not one to argue with women, so I apologise.*

The message he deserved and the message he received are two different things. He deserved: *Shove your apology up your arse and go fuck yourself.* Instead, I let my emotions bleed out and told him how hurtful it was: *You're right though, some things are better left unsaid. I know that now.* The way he turned on me with his venomous tongue was the closure I needed. Yes, I wear my heart on my sleeve. Yes, I have insecurities. Yes, I have flaws. But I'm honest to the core about how I feel, and I don't gamble with peoples' emotions. I'm not sure he could say the same. He had taught me a painful but invaluable lesson.

I don't want you to fucking apologise. I want the guilt to eat you alive. I want you to drown in your thoughts like I drowned in mine.

~Unknown

If I had a penny for every time someone told me, "You were too good for him anyway" or "He was punching above his weight with you, " I'd be rich by now. But to me, they are just useless words and phrases because I've never seen it like that. I don't think anyone is too good for anyone, be it looks-wise, jobwise, money-wise. It's about how you treat someone that makes all the difference. I found out weeks later, Jason had been mocking me on social media and reading out parts of the pages I had sent him to people in the pub. This man left me feeling more embarrassed than I ever thought possible. I would never tear someone apart like that. I've been dealing with my flaws for years on end, so I know what it is to feel shame for the person I am, even if nobody else sees it. To be ridiculed by someone who knows you feel that way is the lowest of the low. I would never stoop to that level and cut someone deep and personally like that. I don't have it in me to be that cruel.

The new layer of skin I had grown was like my walls. Things had spiralled so quickly with Jason, and I hadn't laid the foundations for my defences properly. They were not strong enough yet. My skin wasn't thick enough. He walked in while I was still building them when my skin was brand new, and I was at my most vulnerable. My therapist described what he did as "pissing into an open wound" (*yes, she is brilliant*). I showed him all my cards. I showed him that I would have sex whenever he wanted. I exposed my insecurities, trusted him with my anxiety. He knew I would be there at his beck and call whenever he wanted to see me. Whether he actually had an ounce of guilt that last time he saw me, when he saw me for my trembling anxious self, and couldn't put me through it anymore, I don't know. People that are hurt go on to hurt other people to make themselves feel better. He must have a lot of damage and insecurities himself to need an ego boost like that and to make a joke out of someone's life. The dangerous thing was that he concealed his damage with affection, and I fell hook, line and sinker.

I finally accepted I was battling further deep-rooted issues. That's why I attracted someone with their own turmoil. And what happens when two people like that meet? Their demons fight.

Accepting that was like swallowing a pill without water, scratching my insides and almost impossible to digest. It had been me all along. It was finally time to fight the demon inside me.

Chapter Fourteen
The Heartbreaker… No More

You can't keep dancing with the devil and ask why you're still in hell.

~Unknown

I was starting to worry that I wouldn't be able to have sex again. The more I thought about men, the more they terrified and repulsed me. God has a way with me, though, and with his impeccable timing, I received a worried message from Max. He had heard about my book through the grapevine and asked if he could read his part before it was put to the world. I told him I had plans, but he insisted he would be round at eight o'clock when I was home. I told him I didn't think it was a good idea because we know how it always ends, but he insisted he was only coming to read and even said he would come bearing gifts. "That would be an improvement on all those years ago, " I joked. "A vast improvement, " he agreed. I couldn't believe my eyes as he walked through the front door with my favourite beers and ice cream in tow.

I think no matter how much time passes by, I will always have a weak spot for you. And that terrifies the hell out of me.

~Unknown

He looked better than ever, just like the first time I met him, and was exactly as I remembered. I don't know why he is different from the other men in my life. I never get butterflies when I am around him, and I don't get nervous. I feel calm, like all my worries and anxieties float away.

As we both finished our first beer, he started to read his chapter as I sat there in silence, scared about how he would react. His first thought? That I had forgotten to mention the beautiful model whose virginity he took while we were sleeping together. *Nice.* At least it broke the ice. But what came next caught me off guard. "I still have the letter you wrote to me. I never threw it away."

Why would he tell me that? Why would he still have it after all these years? Is he just going back to his old ways and trying to play a game? Trying to play on those old heart strings of mine again?

"You're off your head, you know, you're a different kettle of fish."

"What do you mean?" I said, with a sharp frown on my face.

"You're just different to anyone else I've met. You wear your heart on your sleeve."

I didn't know if he was complimenting me or criticising me. I told him I can't help but tell everyone that comes into my life what they mean to me or how they've made me feel. I can't keep things to myself. I have never been able to. And then things started to get deeper.

"I am really sorry, you know, " he said, unable to make eye contact as the words left his mouth.

"You fucked me up. You completely broke me, " I blurted out in my croaky voice, realising I was full to the brim with raw emotion.

"I just couldn't be in a relationship with someone that had slept with people I knew. But the worst bit is that it's all my fault. I told everyone how amazing you were in bed, and it backfired because more people wanted to fuck you."

I was shaking by this point. *Was it rage? Disappointment?* Probably a bit of both. "How the fuck do you think that feels?" I asked. "That was how people saw me, a shag."

"You fucked it up for me too though, you told everyone how I was and before I knew it, other women were throwing themselves at me. I got the most attention I ever had when we were sleeping with each other."

It suddenly became apparent that we fucked each other in more ways than one. I could feel the tears building up quickly, so I asked him if he wanted another drink and went to compose myself in the kitchen.

Seeing him will always hurt.

~Unknown

When I came back, not another word was said about our past. We spent the next couple of hours just laughing and talking like the old days, with my head resting comfortably on his legs. I get sucked in so quickly when I am around him. There is no awkwardness. We are just totally at ease with one another. The conversation turned to sex, and I admitted how I struggle to orgasm unless the sex is abusive or a game or fucked up. I saw a glisten in his eye, and I decided that was the perfect opportunity to pounce on him and straddle my legs around him. And just like that, it was as if I jogged his memory, and he told me to go get my box of toys.

I suddenly realised where this would go, swung my legs off him and pretended to walk over to the table for something – telling him no. I said, "I am not doing this, not again." I tried so hard to be stern and stand my ground, but it only took him asking twice and like a giddy schoolgirl, I was upstairs rummaging through the box.

As I came downstairs with a vibrator tucked into the back of my shorts, he pulled one of my dining chairs up to face the sofa. He sat back down and said, "I want you to fuck yourself on that chair, and when you feeling like you're about to cum I want you to stop." Just like that, I was back playing the pathetic submissive I was all those years ago. I slowly pulled my shorts down and slid my lace pants to one side, and placed the vibrator inside of me. Just a minute into what you could only imagine was a show, he leant over, grabbed my pants and ripped them in half in one pull like he did that very first night we met before slumping back into the sofa to watch.

I don't know if it was because it was him I was with or because I was back to being a submissive, but I felt the sudden urge that I was about to orgasm. Out of breath, I told him I couldn't stop, so he grabbed the vibrator and forced me to stop as my legs began to twitch. He told me to start again, but it wasn't long before I couldn't take anymore. I got off the chair, straddled him and told him to put the vibrator inside me. I thought we would kiss again like last time, so I leant in, but he shot me straight down, turned his head and said no. I knew in that very moment I was back to the fucked up situation I was in all those years ago, but I couldn't stop.

The motion of the vibrator going in and out of me got rougher and deeper with each thrust. It was beginning to really hurt as it felt like it would burst through my cervix, but it was the pain that kept me going, the pain I so desperately wanted. There were spots of blood on my cream sofa and his t-shirt. He turned me over, pushed my face up against my living room wall and placed himself and the vibrator inside me, filling both holes. His other hand was wrapped tightly around my hair, pulling it down so my back was fully arched. I could feel sweat dripping down my face, and my breath got shorter and shorter. He let out a deep grunt as he finished inside of me, and as he let go of my hair and took the vibrator out, I let out an even louder "Fuck."

He took himself to the toilet to clean up, and as he walked back into the room, he got dressed and told me he had to leave. I shook my head in disappointment. I knew he would leave the second he got what he wanted.

"Don't be like that. Don't be mardy. I've really got to go."

"Whatever, I knew you would do this, " I said, now rolling my eyes.

He tried to make me laugh, telling me to keep the hat he'd left the last time he was round for good luck. I walked him to the door and waved him off, but I knew this time, as I shut the door behind him, this time was different. I didn't cry. I didn't feel sad. I looked in the mirror in my hallway, and I let out an almighty sigh. A sigh of relief almost. I knew that was the last time I was ever going to see him.

Accepting that was like swallowing a pill without water, scratching my insides and almost impossible to digest. It had been me all along. It was finally time to fight the demon inside me.

Chapter Fifteen
The Realisation

We are all just a bunch of addicts struggling with our drug choice.

~J. M. Storm

Once I mourned my relationship, I discovered there was much more to my healing. The depth of my scar was a lot more extensive than I thought. Max was the last piece of my puzzle. It was as if I needed to go back to the original source to get to the root of my issue; to understand that it was him, it's always been him. I'd feared rejection and judgement all my life because I had never loved myself. When I met Max he fed my fear, turning it into a trauma. Max was the damage I never healed from, and it has haunted me ever since. He is the devil I know, and he created a demon inside me. A demon I'd lain to rest for many years while I was with Chris because there was intimacy and real love there. I think that's why I always went back to Chris, because he never rejected me.

I knew I could turn around and have him with a click of a finger. He loved me so much that he was my safe place. I never had to worry about being rejected by him or him leaving me because I knew he wouldn't. But the second I was single and starved of love, the second I felt rejection, the demon awoke. It started with Max, and conveniently, it had to finish with him. So many of my actions came from him: the posting letters, the heartfelt essays, the abusive sex. He taught me that to keep someone must be through sex, and to give them my body would mean they might fall in love with me. He was the only man who could make me realise the changes I needed to make within myself. Even though these men might have been dickheads, they might have hurt me, and they might have their own toxic traits, it was actually my toxic traits that needed healing. Accepting that was like swallowing a pill without water, scratching my insides and almost impossible to digest. It had been me all along. It was finally time to fight the demon inside me.

I never would have expected you to become my deepest scar yet.

~Unknown

Since I was sixteen years old, I've barely spent a week without a man. I've always had some form of male attention, whether from a relationship, dating someone, sleeping with someone or getting over someone with someone else. I have been self-medicating with male attention for years, and when I think about it, my whole existence has revolved around people and their validation of me. I allowed my life to be based upon other people's approval – or disapproval – of me. I only posted pictures on social media to boost my confidence with comments and likes. I spent hours in the gym building a bigger bum so that I felt sexier to men. I got a boob job and fillers pumped into my lips to look like every other girl.

The list goes on. It's preposterous. I spent so much time feeling like I wasn't good enough, tearing my face, body and personality to shreds, wondering why these men chose other women over me. I can't even count how many times I've heard, "I've always wanted to fuck you" or "I've heard you're so naughty in bed". I always thought this was a compliment. But it damn right is not. It's a fucking insult. It's not "I've always wanted to know the real you, " or "I've always wanted to take you out on a date and treat you right". No, because I allowed myself to live up to people's expectations – good and bad. I was literally a people pleaser (in all senses!) There are not many men out there who have called me intriguing or interesting or told me my smile or laugh is contagious. It's always been "you've got a good arse" or "you're fit". I've been seen as just a sex symbol and not for my soul, and I'm to blame for that. I've used sex as a mask with nearly every man, to stop them from getting to know the real me. I created an image and fed off the attention, and the end result was that I believed it was all I was worth – nothing more and nothing less than my body. It all started to make sense. Why I could never say no to a man when things got intimate, why I never felt like I had the willpower to not have sex, why I thought that giving my game away would make them like me even more. Only that's not how it works. It was no wonder they thought I was easy and someone that doesn't respect herself. You attract what you radiate – I really believe that. I was damaged and needed healing, so I was attracting the male equivalent. I didn't respect myself, and I didn't love myself, so how the hell did I expect any of these men to respect and love me? I didn't want these men to stay, I needed them to – or so I thought. My friend once said to me, "You're one incredible person, Elle. You're one of the funniest, kindest, most beautiful souls I know. You have so much more to give to men than your body." She was right.

The times we love ourselves the least are the times we attract the wrong things into our lives the most.

~April Green

I realise now that's why I'd been reliving the same old story for so long, why I'd always gravitated towards "bad boys". Always wondering who had hurt them and what had happened for them to become so cold, I was always willing to look beyond their past, their hurt and their issues because I craved someone who would do the same for me – to see me for my past and my scars, and love every ounce of me. I loved the idea that I could be this amazing woman who was enough for a man to change. I wanted to be so significant that they'd change their way of life for *me*. And that says it all. It was never about me saving them; it was me who needed saving all along. But the truth is, no man can fix what another man broke. No man can fix the issues you've been carrying since you were a young girl. The men in this book each helped release the tidal wave that had been swirling inside me for years. I was drowning way before I met any of them, and the waters were getting deeper and deeper. It was inevitable that the waves would come crashing down sooner or later. Unfortunately, there are no such things as fairy tales. Prince Charming wasn't going to ride in on his horse and come and rescue me. I had to rescue my goddamn self.

No one can rescue me. I know because I've already tried to get them to do it. It doesn't work. This is all on me.

~Michelle D'Avella

I had to physically unlearn the behaviours that were all attributes of me becoming toxic to myself. My first step, and probably my hardest, was to just be on my own. I completely stopped talking to men and looking for anything. I started to date myself, be in my own company, and my God how I love it now. I watch a film in the bath, even with a side of popcorn sometimes. I go out and buy myself my favourite flowers. Some nights I go to bed at 8pm because I feel like it, and I no longer feel like I'm missing out on life, or hours of scrolling through Instagram. If I feel like having sex, I have sex. With myself. God, that's why they made dildos, right? I'm going to give myself that goddamn orgasm, not a fucking man that doesn't deserve it or probably can't, for that matter. I rarely drink on my own anymore, which has made my mind so much healthier. I've finally hung up my psycho boots. I no longer stalk anyone from my past on social media, or their new followers, for that matter. I am doing me, and quite frankly, they can *do* whoever they want.

You not wanting me was the beginning of me wanting myself.

~Nayyirah Waheed

I also stopped obsessing over my flaws and saw them as positives. My not-so-perky boobs because they fed my child. My C-section scar because that's how Noah was born. My acne scars because I overcame one of the biggest insecurities of my skin. My chest scar from getting rid of a cancerous mole and being alive. When you look at it like that, they are so bloody beautiful, and every day, I now remind myself of this – I make a point of telling myself I'm beautiful when I look in the mirror. Even first thing in the morning when I have dribble down my chin, and my hair looks like it has been electrocuted. Once I started to get in the habit of telling myself these things, drilling them into my mind, it just became the norm and second nature to think that way.

I read a book or started a project if I felt lonely or my mind started to wander. I started doing my house up, something for me and Noah to enjoy. I went back to the gym, and I worked out. I stopped focusing on building a bigger bum and started exercising for what is best for my health.

It's the simple things, like taking a few seconds before I answer a question now, whether it's asked by clients, my parents, friends, anyone. I'm not as irrational as I used to be, and my word vomit is at an all-time low as a result. Most importantly, I say no to things. If I don't feel up to it, or just want to be in my own company, or simply do not want to do something, I say no. As soon as I did it a couple of times, it became a lot easier for me. As soon as I let that pressure go, the thought of having to please everyone all the time was a weight lifted off my shoulders.

And I write. I write and write and write. I journal. Feelings, things that happened that day, whatever is on my mind. It's a place to put it down. To get my thoughts and feelings out. This made me have boundaries. Of course, I still talk to my friends about near enough everything, but writing stopped me from blurting things out to anyone that would listen. I started to become more self-disciplined in oversharing and created boundaries for myself.

Write it out until what hurt you heals.

~Butterflies Rising

I switch off from my phone so much more these days. I try to be more present in my surroundings. Time spent with Noah, time that I'll never get back. With my friends and especially with my parents. Time isn't slowing down, and we don't know how long we have our parents for. I've gone weeks without posting anything on my grid on my Instagram. I just do not need the validation anymore.

I changed what I was doing, not who I am, and that was it. I finally realised it wasn't me that needed changing. It was my behaviours, my reactions, my thinking. Not who I am as a person. And that was when I was finally proud of who I was, when I understood who I am as a person. And that's what self-love is! Accepting myself for who I am and loving all the parts of me that I thought needed changing. Maybe I was crazy, maybe I wasn't, but I am becoming more and more accepting of the person that I am; that I am just someone who feels everything deeply, someone that experiences life very intensely, someone who is very in touch with their emotions, whether that be happy or sad. I'm different. Pain is pain at the end of the day. We are all accustomed to it. Some just feel it more than others. It is such a curse and a blessing to feel the way I do, to remember everything people have said to me, to remember all the little things about someone. But I refuse to change myself for anyone else or because of the fear of judgement.

I am still insecure and sensitive, I still wear my heart on my sleeve, I still care about other people more than I do myself. However, I now know that that doesn't make me weak, and it doesn't make me damaged goods, which is what I used to think. I can't hide away the fact that I'm soft, but it is no longer my weakness. If I took all of that away from me I wouldn't be myself, and the people who love me love me exactly for who I am. I still have bad days. I still have days where I catch myself at the wrong angle, and my mind starts ticking that I need a nose job. Then I think *Elle, for fuck's sake, your nose is perfect the way it is,* and the thought flies away to the back of my brain instead of ticking away. I still have days where I feel emotional and not in total control. The difference is my outlook. It's just a bad day or a bad few hours. It's not a bad life. I allow myself those days. I sit with them and acknowledge them, I try to understand what has triggered it, or I see my therapist.

> *If you want to know what it's like to survive hell and still come out shining brighter than the sun, just look into the eyes of a woman who survived intense damage and refused to allow it to destroy her softness.*
>
> ~Nikita Gill

I no longer feel jealous of anyone that seems "ahead" of me in their life. They are on their journey, and I am on mine. I am in competition with no one. I'm trying my best to learn discipline and control and stick to the path of self-love and self-worth. This is a journey of self-acceptance, and I am telling you now, you will miss out on all the beautiful things life has to offer if you live through other people's eyes. I'm healing and fighting my inner demons. We all have them. Some are stronger than others, and the battle can only be won when we realise how much we want to overcome them. A man, love, sex, a new house, a holiday, plastic surgery: none of those things will make you happy if you aren't happy within yourself. You can search forever, always thinking of the next thing to do to distract you from yourself until you realise it's only you that will heal yourself. It's only you that will heal your scars.

Epilogue

Owning our story and loving ourselves through that process is the bravest thing that we'll ever do.

~Brené Brown

There were nights when I was writing this book or rereading chapters that I wanted to rip the pages out and burn them to ash. There were points where I thought, *OMG, I sound like a psychopath. I can't put that in there. I am going to be so embarrassed. What will people think of me?* But these are my confessions. After all, I can't just skip a chapter and pretend it didn't happen, because it did. It all happened. It's shocking and painful to go back over some of it and remember how I reacted and how much I hated myself. It's almost like reading someone else's story. But it wasn't. It was all me. It is actually sort of heart-warming to know I no longer feel that way.

What people are ashamed of usually makes a good story.

~F. Scott Fitzgerald

I don't know what will happen next. My main trigger has always been rejection, and I know avoiding your triggers isn't healing. So, one day I will put that to the test. For now, I know I'm not quite there yet. I need more time on my own. Everyone's timing for healing is different; some get there faster than others, but I don't want to put myself at risk of relapsing so I will continue to date myself until I feel ready. Maybe I will never know when I am ready. Do any of us really know? Maybe one day someone will come along, see my insecurities and handle me with care. Maybe I'll get my heart shattered again. In fact, I'm certain other men will let me down. The difference is that I won't lose myself again when this happens. I made a promise to myself that I will never ever beg someone to stay in my life again. I will never ask for closure because I don't need it. I have to think, I now know what the fuck I want, and everyone is entitled to that same view, and sometimes you just aren't what another person wants or likes, and that's OK, you aren't made for everyone, and you shouldn't want to be.

Until I'm ready
Let me be
I have to heal myself.

~Samantha King

When I look back at my childhood, I feel warm and fuzzy inside, and my face creases into a smile. I grew up in such a loving family, and any problem I ever faced was solved. And while I wouldn't change it for the world, I was brought up having no resilience. You could say I always got what I wanted, and evidently, if I didn't get what I wanted, I couldn't and didn't know how to cope with it. Now I realise that not getting what we want is a bloody blessing in disguise. I want to pass this message onto Noah. I want my Noah to grow up and make his own mistakes. He will have his own scars that he has to heal from. That's how we learn. It comforts me knowing that as sad as it is, Noah coming from a broken home will teach him resilience. It will teach him that life isn't always perfect and a fairy tale. I will teach him all the lessons I have learnt, and I will sure as hell teach him how to respect women and treat them properly.

I believe that our lives are already planned out for us. Absolutely everything we do is for a reason. It brings me peace, knowing that what is meant to be will never pass me by. I am no longer scared of my future that used to feel so blurry. Yes, I might have no idea what will happen next, but now I see that as something so exciting. Not quite knowing what is around the corner. So maybe soon, I will be brave enough to meet another man and put it to the test. I love myself for always giving love one more chance, for never giving up on it. Love always wins for me! Of course, I want that feeling. I would love flowers on my doorstep, love letters on my windscreen and lying outside watching the stars with someone. I know I have so much to give, but I am not ready to waste it on the wrong person. I am no longer scared of never finding it. I am now more scared I will get so used to being single that I will never want to be in a relationship again, because I'm finally giving *myself* all that love I so desperately wanted.

Maybe I will write another book. Maybe my next book will be about more dating disasters or even me finding love. Maybe it will be about me having the best sex of my life with myself. Who knows, but what I do know is why I wrote this book. It wasn't until I started piecing together these two final chapters that it became very clear that I was writing because it was helping me heal. I was writing because my deep-rooted issues had one scar; a scar that I think I have had for the majority of my life. I thought each of these men had left their own individual scar, but they hadn't. It was just one big wound that was becoming more painful. I had to find the strength to pull the band-aid off the wound, open it up and let the fresh air hit it to heal properly.

Tell the story of the mountain you climbed. Your words could become a page in someone else's survival guide.

~Morgan Harper Nichols

My little advice to you…

I know you want them all to know that they've hurt you. They know this, and they still did it anyway; they just don't care. Don't send the essay, don't send the fucking letter, don't stalk them on social media, don't put the quote up on your feed that is so indirectly directed at them that you may as well tag them in bold italics. Don't watch them online and send yourself crazy. I know for a fact, my darlings, it will. Take your fucking dignity and plant in that pretty little mind of yours that you are so worthy, and it just wasn't meant to be. Don't waste your precious time. Don't waste that limited time that we all have waiting for a guy who hasn't even given you a second thought.

Remember, you are beautiful before any man tells you that you are. Please don't rely on someone's validation of you to believe that you are *the shit*, and if a man doesn't want you, always remember it is their loss. Because these people are not the ones who have to look at your reflection every day, so as long as you know how beautiful you are inside and out, then fuck what anyone else thinks. On that note, there is also so much more to life than beauty and being pretty. Work on having a beautiful heart and a pretty soul.

You do not need a man to survive. You need food and water to survive. You should want a man to complement your life and add to it, not to be your sole reason for living. Because if you rely on someone to live but one day they decide to go, where does that leave you? If you *want* someone and they leave, it's a different story. Sure, it still hurts, but you don't lean on them for your entire happiness. Create your own happiness, remember to live your life whether you are with a man or not. Follow your own dreams, not someone else's.

There is so much more to life than being in a relationship. People need to know this. It's okay if you want to be single until your last dying breath. It's okay if you don't want children. It's okay to be engaged and then not want to get married. It's okay if you were a mum in your teens, and it is bloody well okay to be a single mum. No one thinks the same. We all have different ideas of what life is supposed to be. We have to start living our lives for ourselves, not what people expect us to or what society expects us to. As long as you're happy, then fuck what everyone else is doing.

Sex, alcohol and cigarettes will not save you. They were my saviour for a very long time but eventually, reality kicks in, and self-medicating to numb the pain catches up with you and has the opposite effect. One day, when you least expect it, it will all be bottled up, and you'll explode because you didn't deal with your emotions at the time. It's like pouring your drinks into the same glass without even taking a sip. It won't be long until it's overflowing and making a mess. Sure, have a glass of wine with your girls and cry your heart out, play the sad songs while you're driving along and sing your heart out. Crying is healthy. You're releasing your emotions. You are letting all that pain go. Talk and talk and talk to your friends until their ears feel like they're falling off because that's what they're there for and you would damn well do the same for them. Scream into a pillow, punch a pillow, in fact, hell, smash a plate if you need to! Feel, feel, feel. Then pull yourself together and remember who the fuck you are, and move on. Because we all need to feel. Don't bottle anything up, and always be kind to yourself. In every situation you are going through, look in that mirror, embrace the pain and love yourself through it. It *will* pass.

Don't jump into something until you are healed from your previous relationship or previous trauma because it will always creep up, and you will always carry it on to your next relationship, even years later (I learned this one the hard way). Don't get over someone by getting under someone else. Trust me, it *never* works. Mourn your relationship and work on yourself. Wear that single crown with pride, and just do you!

Date yourself, buy yourself flowers, write yourself love letters, buy yourself sexy as fuck underwear and dance around your bedroom for *you.* Fall in love with yourself first, be your own goddamn rebound.

Lastly, love your scars. I now love my stretch marks on my bum, I love my not-so-perky boobs, I love the little scars on my cheeks and my chest scar, and most of all, I love my caesarean scar. *So* much. I hope you are never ashamed or embarrassed about those scars. I hope you never see them as flaws. I hope you see them as quirks and realise they make you unique. I hope you see that they make you who you are. Scars are just like tattoos but with better stories. They will always be there for a little reminder of what you've been through and what you've overcome. And whether they are visible or not, what happens to scars that are healed properly? They fade with time.

All My Love,
Elle x

Your scars are someone else's signs of hope.

~Danielle LaPorte

Acknowledgements

Thank you for loving me when I still tasted heartache and war.

~Nikita Gill

Thank you to my amazing family for supporting me through this journey. I am so lucky to have you.

To my fabulous friends, I just want to say:

Thank you for staying when others left. Thank you for loving me when I was at my most unlovable. Thank you for being the shoulders I cried on and the hands that wiped away my tears. Thank you for seeing the worst in me. You now get to see the best in me.

Some friends aren't mentioned in this book but still faced the rollercoaster of emotions with me. I am so grateful for you and to every person that has supported me and that has taken their time to read this book. I will forever be in your debt.

And finally, thank you to all the men. I sure as hell couldn't have done it without you.

Printed in Great Britain
by Amazon

69578864R00118